MIDNIGHT AT THE BARCLAY HOTEL

MIDNIGHT AT THE BARCLAY HOTEL

FLEUR BRADLEY

Illustrated by Xavier Bonet

VIKING

VIKING

An imprint of Penguin Random House LLC, New York

First published in the United States of America by Viking,
an imprint of Penguin Random House LLC, 2020

Viking & colophon are registered trademarks of Penguin Random House LLC.

Visit us online at penguinrandomhouse.com

LIBRARY OF CONGRESS CATALOGING-IN-PUBLICATION DATA IS AVAILABLE.

ISBN 9780593202906

Printed in the USA

Book design by Jim Hoover   Typeset in LTC Cloister

1   3   5   7   9   10   8   6   4   2

For my parents,
for raising me surrounded by books

HEDGE MAZE

CUPCAKE SHOPPE

"Enjoy your stay!"

Hours and rates may change upon arrival. Inquire within.

MIDNIGHT AT THE BARCLAY HOTEL

THE INVITATIONS WENT out on Tuesday afternoon, because statistically speaking, that's the best time to offer someone a weekend getaway. Or that's what Mr. Barclay's advisors told him (he had a lot of those). These advisors took very expensive and extensive polling and did research (actually, it was mostly asking random people at the mall). The letters were printed on fancy, thick parchment, the kind of paper that adults use for Very Special Occasions like weddings, or birthday parties with lots of guests and bouncy castles and bands.

But this invitation was not for a party. It was for a weekend at the historic Barclay Hotel. Some said it was haunted, but there was no actual proof. Mr. Barclay owned the hotel, and he had a plan.

He wanted these invitations to be sent out on Tuesday. Five invitations only. No more, no less.

They were delivered by a courier—which was even more expensive than those advisors and the research. This was so that Mr. Barclay could make the whole thing seem important and official. He didn't want anyone to think that this was some sort of scheme! Even though it was. His advisors told him that it's one thing to get a letter in the regular old mail, in the box, mixed in with the grocery store flyer and the electric bill. It's quite another to get a letter with a real embossed seal to close the envelope, delivered by a courier, where you have to sign for it. So mysterious.

Five envelopes, with five invitations. Mr. Barclay guessed that there would be some stragglers—there always were. But the five main guests had been chosen carefully. A cowboy, a librarian, a CEO (that stands for chief executive officer—which is a big deal), an actress, and a detective all got their invitations that Tuesday.

Dear [insert esteemed guest's name here],

Congratulations! You are a winner. "What did I win?" you might ask. An all-expenses-paid weekend getaway to the historic Barclay Hotel, from Friday, April 3, through Sunday, April 5.

From the moment you arrive, you will find yourself enchanted by the newly renovated dining hall, where you will feast on a five-course meal included in your prize winnings.

Enjoy the (also newly renovated!) indoor pool, hot tub, bowling alley, and extensive multilevel library if you fancy an afternoon read by the fireplace. All meals and entertainment (expect surprises!) are included in your stay. Did we mention it's all expenses paid?

We will see you promptly at five o'clock Friday evening to start your glorious getaway!

RSVP by Thursday to Gregory Clark, butler of the Barclay Hotel.

DISCLAIMER: The pool and hot tub may or may not be open. The Barclay Hotel is not responsible for any encounter you may have with vermin, errant staff, wonky elevators, leaky ceilings, ghosts, or unstable antiques. Cellular phone service is not available at the Barclay Hotel. Do not use the white room towels for pool attendance; bring your own pool towel. Five-course meal may actually be a one-course meal. There is no room service available at the Barclay Hotel.

Not everyone read the fine print—not when there was a free vacation at stake. Some guests read it later, but by then it was too late.

No, each and every one of the five people invited felt very special when they received the letter, even if not all of them were all that excited to go. *Congratulations! You are a winner*, the letter said.

Everyone likes to be a winner. Mr. Barclay counted on it.

PART I

LIARS, LIARS

or, The Players

JJ WASN'T SUPPOSED to read the letter, but he did anyway. He couldn't resist the thick paper and the chance to break the seal on the back of the envelope. It all looked so important. You really couldn't blame him. His mom had already forgotten about the letter and left it unopened on the kitchen counter. She rarely had time for anything these days.

JJ, on the other hand, had nothing but time.

He had just gotten out of school, and Tuesday was his most hated day of the week. He was always forced to go to Book Club and Battle of the Books, which was like the grand master of misery for those who are not into books. JJ didn't like reading very much (that's an understatement—he despised it, everything about it, from the quietness to the dancing letters and the book reports afterward).

What JJ really loved was ghost hunting. He got excited at the thought of collecting evidence of haunting activity with his infrared camera, voice recorder, and electromagnetic field (that's EMF for short) detector. The camera would catch temperature fluctuations, since ghosts show up as cold spots. The voice recorder could catch a ghost's voice (this was harder, JJ thought), and the EMF detector would reveal a ghost's electrical current—the detector would spike. Ghost hunting can be exciting or monumentally boring, depending on how the ghosts are feeling that day.

The week before the invitation came, JJ and his friend Tristan had caught signs of a (possible) haunting in the attic. JJ lived in an old house that made squeaky noises and had lots of dark, mysterious corners. But JJ had reason to believe that those little orbs he and Tristan caught on camera were not dust. The EMF detector spiked, and there was some garbled noise on the voice recorder—

sure indicators that a ghost was present. You never knew what evidence you might find. It was why JJ loved ghost hunting.

And now there was this envelope, on a regular (most hated) Book Club Tuesday. Unfortunately, JJ's dad was an English professor at the local college, and he loved all things books, which was why his dad had volunteered to run the Book Club and Battle of the Books at Aspen Springs Middle School. It made the whole situation with JJ hating books a little sticky.

JJ could hear his mom on the phone in the other room. *Just troubleshoot it, guys, just troubleshoot it.* It was her favorite phrase. JJ's mom was very good at her job as CEO—a little *too* good, if you asked JJ. He wished she would take a break from her phone every once in a while.

JJ scratched his mop of curly red hair as he read the invitation.

Jackie Jacobson was written in cursive letters across the front of the envelope. It looked like the writer had used one of those old-fashioned ink pens. JJ couldn't resist. He looked at the letter, read it twice (except for that tiny print—you needed a magnifying glass to read that). And smiled to himself.

This was his moment.

Around the same time that JJ found the envelope addressed to his mother, he'd been hatching a plan to convince his parents to let him visit the spookiest places in Aspen Springs, Colorado. The Barclay Hotel was at the top of the list of most haunted places within a twenty-mile radius of his house. The trouble was it had been closed for years. No one was allowed in. Not even professional ghost hunting crews.

Even JJ's favorite online show, *Ghost Catchers*, had tried and failed. This guy named Hatch (even his name was cool) would go to haunted locations and investigate. Hatch had been to Alcatraz, the Winchester Mystery House, and a whole bunch of other creepy places. But never to the Barclay Hotel. The show had tried to get access (they even just showed up once), but the owner, Mr. Barclay, always declined.

And here was an invitation, a fancy one at that, to give

JJ access to the place for a whole entire weekend. He could ghost hunt while he was there!

Maybe he'd even send his video footage and other evidence (there had to be lots!) to Hatch, and then JJ would definitely be invited on the show. And then maybe his parents wouldn't think ghost hunting was "silly fake science" (his mom's words) anymore.

Access to the Barclay Hotel—for a whole weekend, no less. An opportunity like this one comes along rarely. Once in a lifetime, one might say.

"Are you ready for Book Club, JJ?"

"Did you see this?" he asked his dad, waving the invitation.

His dad squinted (he really needed glasses but was avoiding a trip to the eye doctor). "An invitation?"

"Mom won a trip to the Barclay Hotel."

JJ's dad smiled. "How fun."

"I want to go to the Barclay Hotel," JJ blurted out, knowing that with parents, it was better to tell them what you actually wanted sometimes. Except when it came to

Book Club. "And you know Mom owes me one."

JJ had been saving this IOU for a few months now, waiting for the best opportunity. See, JJ's mom was always so busy running her restaurant franchise (PB&JJ— because everything's better with peanut butter!) that sometimes she missed important stuff, like parent-teacher conferences, award ceremonies, and science fairs.

Not that JJ was an award-y kind of kid. But there had been an art exhibit back in December that his mom was supposed to come see. And she'd missed it, because she had a PB&JJ emergency in Kansas. JJ's mom apologized—a lot—and gave JJ a big IOU.

He decided it was time to cash it in.

"BUT I DON'T have time for this," JJ's mom said once she got off the phone. They were all in the kitchen: JJ's dad was putting on his shoes, and JJ held the envelope while his mom was reading the invitation.

Again.

She sighed and let her fingers run over the heavyweight white paper. She flipped the letter over, even though it was blank. Maybe she thought there was a way out written on the back.

"But you owe me," JJ reminded her. "You said anything I want, anytime, no questions asked." This kind of IOU was only given out on those rare occasions when parents truly messed up.

His mom said, "I heard Mr. Barclay is allergic to peanut butter."

"So?" JJ asked.

"He won't like PB&Js," his mom said. It was a weak argument, everyone knew that.

JJ tried to think of something to persuade his mom.

His dad spoke up. "The invitation says that there's a hot tub. You love those, Jackie." He winked at JJ. Despite all the bookishness, his dad could be pretty cool sometimes. Now JJ was feeling bad that he'd been ghost hunting around the house when he told his dad he was reading . . .

"I *do* love those," his mom said. Most adults are suckers for hot tubs. It's like going swimming without making an effort.

Jackie read the invitation again, but only briefly glanced over the fine print. If she'd read carefully, she might have noticed that she'd be cut off from the world. No cell phone service.

Plus, Jackie had a secret, one her family didn't know

about—not even her husband. And we all know what it feels like to keep a secret that big.

This invitation could be a way to honor that IOU and keep her secret, Jackie figured. So she said, "Okay."

JJ smiled.

He would regret coming to the Barclay Hotel, especially Saturday evening, when everything went all wrong. When his own secret was out—the one he'd been hiding from his parents for a while now.

But right then, JJ was so excited, he high-fived his mom. He didn't even mind going to Book Club—he might even try to read a few pages. That's how excited JJ was to go to the Barclay Hotel.

MEANWHILE, WAY OUTSIDE of town inside a big barn out on a hundred-acre ranch, a cowboy named Buck Jones was saddling up a horse named Lemon Drop. She had been his best friend ever since she broke out of the pasture next door, which housed a mustang rescue. The horse tried to steal a lemon drop right from his hand! After that, Buck adopted her, and the rest was history.

Cowboy Buck loved being one with the land. It was all he wanted: to be outside in Colorado, herding his cattle and riding Lemon Drop.

Buck rode Lemon Drop to meet the courier, and to sign for his invitation, the one on the fancy paper. Now Buck turned it over in his hands and considered accepting it. He'd been to the Barclay estate just a few days ago to talk to Mr. Barclay. But the conversation quickly turned sour (much like a lemon drop, but without the joy). Buck adjusted the straps on the saddle while he thought about whether he should go or not.

After what happened the other day, he wasn't exactly on good terms with Mr. Barclay. Buck had called the man a few names—from afar, but still. They were sparring, that was the truth.

Not that Buck Jones was on particularly good terms with the truth, not by a long shot. He was a liar, he knew that. He lied every day, about owning the ranch—

Well, it was better just not to think too long on this nasty business. His last visit to Mr. Barclay in particular.

The thing was, Buck had a dream for the ranch: a horseback-riding stable and candy store. People could come ride horses and then pick out candy as they passed the displays. His horse Lemon Drop gave him the idea, and Buck thought it was brilliant. Buck would call it the Lemon Drop Shop. Horses and candy—who wouldn't love to come visit?

But making a dream like that come true was difficult, to say the least. The ranch needed tending to every day: the fences needed repairs; the stables were showing their age. And the cattle needed herding. Ranching was hard work. And the thought of opening a candy store on top of that? Forget about it!

Buck hadn't been on vacation for years. A little break from the ranch could be nice. This five-course meal sounded delicious, and Buck (despite being a rugged cowboy) really liked a refined meal from time to time. But if he accepted the invite, would he be able to keep his secret?

Of course he would, Buck told himself. He was a cowboy, and they kept secrets like nobody's business. They knew when to be silent, and when to ride away from trouble (preferably on their favorite horse).

Buck got in the saddle, popped a lemon drop in his mouth, and adjusted his cowboy hat. It was decided: he was going to the Barclay Hotel that weekend.

Would he regret it later? Well, you can guess the answer to that . . .

IN THE TOWN of Aspen Springs, teen and children's librarian Ms. Chelsea Griffin was in her home library, sitting in her oversize chair, having a cup of afternoon tea with lots (and lots) of honey in it. Ms. Chelsea needed a little comfort, after the excitement of the previous week.

On her coffee table, there was her teapot and the letter, folded next to the envelope with the broken seal. Ms. Chelsea had read the letter twice, but much like everyone else, she hadn't read the fine print. She'd set the letter down, picked it up again, and studied the (clearly bona fide) seal on the envelope.

She'd hoped she'd won something big when the letter came—by courier, requiring her signature. Ms. Chelsea played the lottery and just about every contest you could find. At the young age of twenty-four, she had to be careful with her money. Being a teen (and children's—she was a multitasker) librarian didn't pay as much as she'd hoped.

When Ms. Chelsea got the fancy letter, she thought it might be prize money. Almost daily, Ms. Chelsea diligently filled out entry forms at those festivals in town, in her magazines, and online. But so far, she'd only won a bowling ball at the county fair last year. And she didn't like bowling, not even with the bumpers on the sides.

But now Ms. Chelsea had actually won something nice: a weekend away. Only it was at the Barclay Hotel, the last place she should be seen. Because Ms. Chelsea—despite her status as librarian, a most trusted position—was a liar, just like the other invited guests for the weekend. She had a secret to keep.

A whopper of a secret.

Ms. Chelsea was nervous. A little scared, you could say, and everyone knows librarians are never scared. It takes nerves of steel to be a librarian.

She read the letter one last time, sipping her super-sweet tea before picking up the phone to RSVP. There really was no choice: she had to go, if she wanted to make sure her secret was kept. Plus, Ms. Chelsea had a dream—not for herself, of course, but for the library. She hoped for an elaborate extension to the kids' section, with arcade games where you could win books, a giant slide (who didn't like whirling down with their hands in the air?), and maybe even a locomotive that looped around the building. It was a bold and crazy plan . . .

Ms. Chelsea sighed. Aside from her dreams of expanding the library's children's department, all she wanted was to share stories with the kids. There was nothing like that spark when a kid read a book and was swept away by the story—just like she was when she was reading. Books were magic to Ms. Chelsea. She wanted to share that with the world.

But it was an uphill battle, being a librarian.

Maybe this weekend away would be a nice break, she told herself. *Maybe I'll bring my bowling ball.*

No one could possibly find out her secret if she was bowling.

RETIRED DENVER METRO area detective Frank Walker received the letter like the other guests, on Tuesday. He'd been in the middle of watching *Antiques Roadshow*—it was his favorite because Detective Walker loved the stories. Who wouldn't enjoy finding a hidden treasure in the attic or at a flea market? He went to garage sales every weekend, but so far all he'd been able to pick up were a few trinkets, none worth anything substantial.

So when the invitation came, Detective Walker felt like a real winner. He rubbed his bald, dark brown head and couldn't resist a little smile.

"What's that?" Penny asked. His granddaughter was

visiting from Florida for the week and had a giant stack of books in front of her, waiting to be read. Penny was curled up on the couch, her tiny frame taking up just the smallest corner. Her dark skin made her eyes look extra bright as she tried to see what was on the paper. "That letter looks fancy." She wrinkled her nose to push her glasses up.

"It's an invitation," Detective Walker said. He handed Penny the letter.

She grinned as she read it. "You're a winner, Grandpa! It says so right here." Penny's face lit up. "What's this Barclay Hotel?"

"It's famous," Detective Walker answered. "They say it's haunted."

Penny grabbed her phone and let her fingers dance across the screen. "Sure is. Says here it's the top haunted location in Colorado. And"—her face lit up even more when she shared this—"it has the largest private library in the state of Colorado."

Unlike JJ, Penny loved to read. She could spend hours at the library, getting lost in the stacks like there was a treasure hunt and she was the explorer. In fact, her parents often had to pick her up at her local library after it closed, because Penny would forget about time. She made getting lost in a book an art form.

Detective Walker took the letter back, and read it again. There had to be a catch somewhere, a kink in the cable . . . You don't just win a weekend getaway without entering a contest somewhere.

Penny *did* read the tiny print, unlike the other invited guests. "Says there's no cell phone service."

"Huh." Detective Walker considered this. No cell

phones. That seemed like a nice break anyway: just peace and quiet.

But then he hesitated. In the back of the detective's mind, there was a tiny alarm bell going off—it was his detective's hunch, telling him that something about this invitation was off. But he also imagined himself having the relaxing spa weekend of his dreams . . .

"Can we go?" Penny asked.

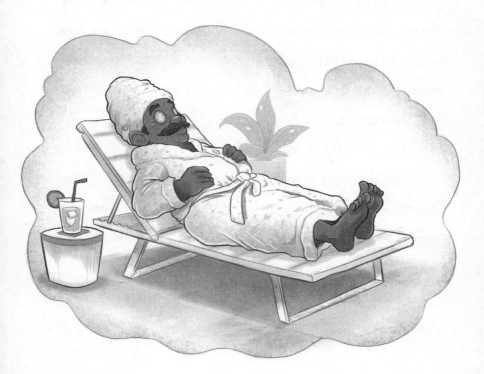

Now, Penny didn't ask for much when she visited. She'd go along on all Detective Walker's garage sale hunts, she'd watch *Antiques Roadshow*, and she'd eat whatever he cooked (which wasn't very fancy) without complaining. Even when her grandpa made broccoli casserole.

These trips to Colorado were a much-needed break for Penny. Her parents owned a scuba diving school, and while that may sound super fun to everyone else, Penny would rather spend her time reading and drawing (she was getting quite good) than swimming underwater. She was afraid of a lot of things; being underwater was somewhere near the top of her fear list. But a giant library? Now, that sounded amazing. . . .

"Please . . . ?" Penny asked again.

The detective hesitated. His daughter had told him specifically to keep things quiet. Apparently, Penny was prone to panicking lately. But Detective Walker really wanted to go too. He was a winner, finally.

He paused to ponder the decision for a moment longer.

"I like this 'no cell phone reception' business," Detective Walker mumbled. "Says here there's a hot tub."

Secretly (or not so secretly, because Penny knew all about it) he really wanted a pampered getaway. Being a detective for several decades had given Detective Walker a crick in his neck, and a good massage sounded like a dream.

"I'll bet there's a spa too, with salt scrubs and massages and mud facials," Penny said, basically reading his mind. She had no idea if this was actually true (for the record, it wasn't), but she really wanted to go to the Barclay Hotel, so she went along with the dream.

Detective Walker smiled. "You think they'll put those little cucumber slices on my eyes?" he asked. "I've always wanted to try that."

"Of course," Penny said, nodding. "And we can take nice long walks around the grounds, eat some fancy food."

The detective was silent. Penny knew he just needed a little nudge to say yes.

"Can we go, *please*, Grandpa?" Penny gave him her

best pleading face. It was a good one, with sad-dog eyes.

"You're not afraid of the ghosts at the Barclay Hotel?" he asked her.

"Poppycock," Penny said with a smile. That means "nonsense." It was their word—Grandpa and Penny's. They'd heard it on *Antiques Roadshow* and laughed at the sound. Then it became their thing. Grandpa and Penny were both just-the-facts kind of people.

He glanced at the invitation one more time. "Oh, why not," he said, and made the call to RSVP. Penny cheered and rushed off to start packing her bags, imagining the hours she was going to spend in the Barclay Hotel library.

Detective Walker was the only guest with no secrets. Later, he would realize why he was at the Barclay Hotel and why he'd been chosen. It was exactly *because* he had no secrets. And because everyone else on the guest list had secrets to spare.

Even Penny had a secret, something she hadn't told even her grandpa, and she pretty much told him everything. They were two peas in a pod, her mom liked to say. When she wasn't visiting, Penny called her grandpa at least once a week, to talk books, detective TV shows, and yard sale hunting.

But this secret she kept in her heart, like the twist in a good mystery book. Maybe someday she'd share it—but for now, she had a trip to prepare for!

IT WAS FRIDAY morning at the Barclay Hotel, and
Emma had just gotten the saddest news you can possibly
imagine. Emma had been moping around the hotel for
days. As amazing as the hotel was, she'd been just too
upset (more on why later). And now she was getting tired
of her own sadness.

On top of that, Emma was extra bored that Friday.
Sure, the Barclay Hotel had plenty to do for a twelve-year-
old girl: there was the pool, the movie theater, the carousel, the Cupcake Shoppe, and the bowling alley. And the
elevator had this great game that—well, that was kind of
a Barclay Hotel secret.

But Emma didn't want any of those things. Really, she just wanted another kid to hang out with.

Emma spent most of her downtime roaming the hotel. Her parents had other things to do, so she hung out in the kitchen with her uncle, Chef Pierre. But even he couldn't talk to her.

That Friday morning, she'd already roamed the halls and watched Chef Pierre cook oatmeal for breakfast (with raisins, very grown-up and dull). And now she was sitting on a porch rocker, pushing her feet against the squeaky old floorboards.

Back and forth, back and forth.

Squeak, squeak. So boring!

Emma twisted a strand of long dark hair around her finger, and faced the sun. She could use a little daylight. Too much time in the hotel this winter had made her kind of pale.

Mr. Clark, the butler, stepped outside, followed by her uncle. Both men had their eyes on the blue sky and hadn't seen Emma outside.

"Do you think it will snow?" Mr. Clark asked.

"*Je ne sais pas*," her uncle replied. He was French, and often forgot that other people were not. He quickly switched to English. "I don't know. The weather forecast said only ten percent chance."

Mr. Clark nodded. "That's acceptable. Plus, no one can control the weather."

"*Mais oui*—that's right, monsieur."

"Before I forget: it appears we have a straggler. Two stragglers, in fact. Kids, to make matters worse."

The chef's face was like a giant question mark.

"A straggler is someone who tags along and hangs behind the real invited guest, an extra person . . ."

"Ah, *oui*."

"A boy, aged twelve," Mr. Clark said. "And a girl— she's eleven. Two of our guests RSVP'd asking to bring their kids."

"I'll count it into the food preparations," the chef said. "Perhaps pancakes for dinner?" Emma's uncle specialized in pancakes, pizza, hot dogs, and burgers—food kids like.

"No more children's food, Pierre," Mr. Clark said with a sigh. "Please."

The chef nodded but couldn't hide his disappointment.

"It's important that this weekend goes off without a hitch, you understand, Pierre?" Mr. Clark said to the chef. "We have to keep our plan on track."

"*Oui.*" His voice was small.

Emma's ears perked up, but she didn't say anything. What plan could they be talking about? When you're eavesdropping on grown-ups, it's better to keep your lips zipped. Any kid knows that.

"Back to work, then." The butler turned, and went back inside the mansion.

The chef let out a big sigh. Emma didn't want to call attention to herself, so she sat very still in her rocker until her uncle followed Mr. Clark inside.

Emma was so excited—there were stragglers coming! A twelve-year-old boy and an eleven-year-old girl, Mr. Clark had said. And Emma knew what that meant.

Friends.

All the plans Mr. Barclay had made, everything that had been set in motion, the whole invitation business—Emma didn't know and couldn't care less about it all. There were two kids her age coming to the Barclay Hotel.

Things were about to be so much less boring. Maybe not boring at all.

JJ MADE SURE his mom RSVP'd. Every day, he reminded her of the trip they were taking on Friday. On Wednesday, he placed her small suitcase by the closet. On Thursday, he left sticky notes on her mirror, on the fridge, and by her phone.

THREE P.M. FRIDAY
BARCLAY HOTEL
BRING JJ

Once upon a time, before JJ's mom became a big-shot CEO of her own company, she would help JJ with his sight words for school. They were a list of words sent home every week that he was supposed to remember just by looking at them, so reading went faster. This was hard for JJ.

So his mom came up with a game where they would take three words from the list and turn them into a story every day. By the end of the week, they usually had the word list used up, and JJ had an easier time remembering them. Mostly because of all the crazy stories.

Like SUDDENLY, PINK, and CAPTAIN.

Or BREAKFAST, CIRCUS, and UMBRELLA.

These words made for some fun stories.

That Friday, JJ was packed and ready to go at two o'clock. JJ's secret was still safe, and his dad had left him a book for the weekend. *The History of the Barclay Hotel.* It was fat (four hundred pages!) and looked super boring. He stuffed it in the bottom of his backpack.

JJ also packed his basic ghost hunting kit: the voice recorder, the EMF detector, his infrared camera, a logbook, and a flashlight. He was ready to catch some ghosts.

JJ even packed some extra gear—you can never be too prepared. He had three tripods, which he borrowed from his friend and fellow ghost hunter Tristan, because if he did see a ghost, he wanted to make sure he got the best angle. JJ brought three reels of power cables, just in case the nearest outlet was far away from the ghost. He couldn't expect the ghost to cater to the needs of his camera. He brought his laptop, a pad of sticky notes, four extra notebooks, and five pens, because—

Well, the ghost hunting life is unpredictable. He fit *all* his ghost hunting gear into two giant suitcases he found in the attic.

JJ was ready.

When his mom had called to RSVP, the estate manager told her that the Barclay Hotel would send a car to the house to pick them up. This made the whole thing even fancier, and JJ was extra excited.

Now it was Friday, two thirty, and JJ began to worry. At two forty, JJ texted her.

THREE P.M.! BARCLAY HOTEL! BRING JJ!

No reply. And at three o'clock sharp, the doorbell rang. This was the car service, and his mom still wasn't here.

He rushed downstairs, with his backpack and the invitation in hand. The suitcases were parked neatly by the front door.

The driver, dressed in black and wearing dark sunglasses, looked very serious. "Are you JJ Jacobson?"

JJ gulped and then gave a quick nod. How was he going to stall this serious-looking man until his mom was there?

The suitcases. "Hang on, I have more," he told the driver. JJ darted back into the house and rolled the last piece of luggage outside.

The driver looked at JJ and then back at the car.

"Hold up, kid," the driver said with a frown. "I can't fit that in there. Small luggage only."

JJ looked back at his two giant suitcases. "Are you sure?" he asked the driver. "I was thinking we could tie them to the roof . . . ?"

The man gave one stern shake of the head.

"Okay." Now JJ frantically racked his brain for ways to stall the driver until his mom got there. "My mom isn't here yet, but she should be here any second."

The driver looked over his shoulder at the car.

The back window lowered and his mom waved. "Three p.m., right? I got your notes."

JJ smiled. This weekend was going to be great!

IN THE MIDDLE of Aspen Springs, off Patterson Avenue, our fifth and last invited guest, Ms. Fiona Fleming, was only just opening up her invitation. She was a young actress and part-time spiritual medium, very busy busy busy (with what, no one was entirely sure), so after she signed for the letter on Tuesday, she just dropped it on her desk. Despite being only twenty-four years old, Fiona was overwhelmed by life.

And Fiona was too busy worrying about her secret. It was paralyzing her, honestly, and that was not a good thing for an actress. She just had to snap out of it.

It was now Friday, and Fiona was finally taking a step back from her long week.

Just thinking about the horrible, horrible drama she was dealing with (and not the drama of the theater or spiritual medium kind) made her heart race. This weekend at the Barclay Hotel might be just the thing she needed to take care of her problems.

Plus, it would give her an in. A front-row seat, if you will, to find out if her secret was still safe. Fiona couldn't resist a good theater pun.

How Fiona loved the theater! She could be anyone she wanted on the stage, but theater had cost her a lot. *Too much.* She hadn't been there when her father died, because she was in the middle of a tour. By the time she'd learned of his passing, she was somewhere in Iowa and had to rush home to even make it to the funeral.

Sad, to say the least. Fiona missed her father.

Now there was this trip, an invitation to cover her tracks, perhaps. It practically fell into her lap (well, it was delivered to her door, to be more precise).

She frantically dialed the number on the invitation and crossed her fingers and her toes (while sitting down, otherwise she might topple over) as the phone rang.

Twice. Three times.

"Barclay Hotel, this is Gregory Clark, the butler."

"Really? Mr. Clark?" Fiona was confused. It will become clear why later.

"Yes, really." The man cleared his throat. "To whom am I speaking?"

"Um, okay then." Fiona fumbled with the letter, dropping it and looking at the name again—it was indeed Mr. Clark she was to RSVP to. "I apologize for being so tardy in my response. This is Fiona Fleming." When there was a silence, she added, "Of Voilà! On Stage Productions. And spiritual medium to the wealthy."

There was a silence on the other end of the line, and it was making her anxious.

"You invited me. 'You are a winner.' It says so. Right here in the letter." Fiona tried her best not to seem out of breath, but she really was quite desperate.

The man on the other end cleared his throat again. "You are late."

"I know."

There was more silence, and Fiona almost gave in to the urge to fill it when Gregory Clark said, "Very well. Mr. Barclay is eager for you to join us, and I would not want to disappoint him."

His accent was very British, and Fiona responded in an almost British accent, "Oh jolly good."

"Are you mocking me, Ms. Fleming?"

"No, no!" She composed herself and uncrossed her fingers and toes. "I'm an actress, I'm just always . . . practicing."

Mr. Clark did not sound impressed. "The car will pick you up at four p.m. sharp, Ms. Fleming. Don't be late."

Fiona was about to tell him she would be ready with her suitcase, but the line went dead. Just as well. She had to hurry, to gather her costumes for the weekend. This was her chance to fix her mistakes and make things right. Talk to Mr. Barclay, perhaps, about her play.

Plus, Fiona Fleming had a show to put on.

AND THERE YOU have it, folks: librarian Chelsea, CEO Jackie Jacobson, cowboy Buck, actress Fiona, and Detective Walker. Plus our two kid stragglers, JJ and Penny, all ready for one prize weekend getaway.

It's about time we got to the Barclay Hotel.

PENNY AND DETECTIVE Walker stood outside his small house, ready for their ride to the Barclay Hotel. The driver was exactly on time—something the detective could appreciate. Punctuality was an underrated quality.

Penny clutched her book bag and bounced on her heels. This trip was so exciting! She couldn't wait to take lots of pictures, so she could show her friends when she got home to Florida. Maybe for once everyone wouldn't assume that all she did was read.

The car was long, like a limo of some sort. Penny had never been in a limo before. She wanted to take pictures, but there wasn't time to pull out her phone. The driver held the door, looking all official in his suit and hat.

There were two benches facing each other. A woman sat on the forward-facing part. She was on the phone talking about troubleshooting things. And there was a boy. Penny guessed he was about her age. He clutched a backpack on his lap, like it held a treasure or something.

"Hi," Penny said as she slid to the far end of the rear-facing seat. Her legs dangled off the seat but couldn't touch the ground. She'd never liked being short; it made her feel like a toddler.

Her grandpa slid in. He looked perturbed. "I hope I don't get carsick, facing backward," he muttered.

"You can sit up front if you like," the driver offered.

The detective hesitated. He looked at Penny, clearly worried about her sitting alone.

"It's fine, Grandpa," Penny said. She put her book bag next to her. "It's not a long drive."

The detective nodded, and moved to the front of the car on the passenger side.

"I'm JJ," the boy said. "Did you win too?"

Penny nodded. "My grandpa did. I'm tagging along."

"Me too." JJ pointed to his mother. "Sorry, my mom's always busy."

"I get it. My parents are like that sometimes too," Penny said. If they weren't running their business, they were underwater in their scuba gear. "I'm Penny."

There was an uncomfortable silence. They drove up some winding roads—because she was facing backward, Penny couldn't really tell much from what she saw out her window. There were lots of pine trees, and she could feel that they were going up in elevation. It made her a little dizzy. The altitude took some getting used to, and they were obviously going high up into the mountains.

JJ said, out of the blue, "Do you think the Barclay Hotel is haunted?" He seemed very excited to go, just like Penny.

Penny hesitated. "I don't know . . ."

"Do you ever watch *Ghost Catchers*?"

Penny shook her head. She was about to tell JJ that she did watch a lot of *Antiques Roadshow*, but she thought that might make her sound boring.

"It's pretty good." JJ thought it was a great show, but didn't want to seem too eager. Penny could tell by the way he was trying to hide his excited expression. "They go to these haunted places and try to get evidence of ghosts."

Penny almost rolled her eyes. "Like what evidence?"

JJ sat up a little. "There was an apparition, a ghost, and they caught it on camera at this old tavern in Maine. And then they got a voice recording of a spirit telling them to go away."

Penny seemed to think that over for a second. "How about the Barclay Hotel? What's the story there?"

JJ said, "Supposedly, there's a lady in a white night-dress who roams the halls of the hotel. They say she's Mr. Barclay's wife, looking for her daughter."

"That's kind of sad," Penny said.

"I know." JJ paused. "And there's a little boy who died there, way back in, like, the nineteen fifties or something. He was the son of one of the hotel's guests. They say he sometimes plays in the halls with his marble collection."

"Who is *they*?" Penny asked. She really didn't believe in all this ghost stuff. Poppycock, that's what it was.

"Employees of the Barclay Hotel," JJ said.

This didn't seem like very strong evidence to Penny, but JJ was clearly excited.

He continued, "There's this creepy ghost caretaker named Mr. Roberts who floats around outside. And then there's room two seventeen, of course—the most haunted room in the hotel . . ."

Suddenly, JJ squinted. "You don't believe in ghosts. You're a skeptic."

Penny shrugged. "I just don't think it's real."

JJ clutched his backpack. "Well, I'm going to investigate this weekend. I'm a ghost hunter."

"How do you even do that? Hunt for ghosts, I mean." Penny was a little curious now. She liked investigating things. It's why she loved going to the library: there was always something new to discover.

JJ said, "I have a ghost hunting kit." He looked at Penny. "I still have to investigate more about the hotel history. That's part of ghost hunting too: doing research." He unzipped his backpack and pulled out a giant book. It had a picture of the Barclay Hotel on it, surrounded by a gilded frame. JJ handed the book to Penny.

The History of the Barclay Hotel.

"Wow, this thing weighs as much as I do," Penny said. It was no exaggeration. She opened it, and saw the tiny print, with only a few black-and-white photos throughout.

"Boring," JJ said.

"But I'll bet it has good information on the hotel," Penny countered. "Research. That part sounds interesting." Penny got tossed around as they made a sharp turn one way, then another. She held on as best as she could. The book actually helped weigh her down.

"I hope I get to stay in room two seventeen," JJ said.

Penny handed the book back. She thought about JJ's ghost hunting, and his investigation. And she thought about her own goal: to have a story to tell when she got home. And not one from a book this time. "I'll make you a bet," she said. "I bet I can prove that the Barclay Hotel isn't haunted."

That was quite the gamble.

JJ raised his chin. "You're on."

Just as Penny was feeling like she might get carsick, the driver slowed. From her window, she saw a massive clearing appear between the pine trees, like a surprise.

Or a secret rather, hidden in the Rockies.

There it was!

The Barclay Hotel.

9

THE BARCLAY HOTEL was even more impressive than the photos. The front porch was massive and ran the length of the white clapboard building. There were large identical turrets to the left and right, making the place look like a castle.

The driver stopped at the front of the hotel on the gravel driveway.

Penny was awestruck. She was craning her neck to peek through the car window, and JJ noticed that her legs weren't touching the ground.

"This place is amazing, isn't it?" Penny said. All JJ could do was nod in agreement. He still couldn't believe he was here!

JJ's mom frowned. "My call dropped."

"There's no cell phone service at the Barclay Hotel, ma'am," the driver said. Penny remembered this from reading that teeny tiny print on the invitation, because she had been paying attention.

Jackie's eyes went wide.

"Is there Wi-Fi?" Jackie asked. Her voice sounded strained.

The driver shook his head as he got out and opened the door for them. "Mr. Barclay believed the hotel should be an escape from the outside world."

"Which Mr. Barclay are you talking about?" JJ asked. See, JJ was a sharp kid. He noticed the driver was talking about Mr. Barclay in the past tense. "Must be Mr. Barclay Senior, the owner's father. Right?"

The driver didn't respond. He just took Jackie's suitcase out of the trunk and set it on the gravel. Penny's grandpa got his own bag and observed the hotel with a smile.

JJ's mom stared at her cell phone for a long moment, then looked up at the Barclay Hotel as she let out a sigh.

"That hot tub had better be good," she mumbled.

But JJ wasn't going to let his mom's frustration ruin his weekend. He was at the Barclay Hotel!

A man walked out onto the porch. He was tall, wearing a dark suit with a striped vest, and a chain that disappeared into his pocket. His shoes were shiny, and he had a red bow tie and a very, *very* big mustache. If you were a mustache expert, you'd recognize it as a handlebar mustache. "Welcome to the Barclay Hotel, Mrs. Jacobson," the mustached man said. "I'm the butler, Mr. Clark." He looked down his nose at JJ. "And this must be your son."

"Yes, this is JJ. I mentioned I was bringing him when I RSVP'd," Jackie said. Sometimes, JJ really loved his mom's bossy CEO attitude. Like right then.

"And I assume this is your granddaughter, Detective Walker?" the butler asked Penny's grandpa.

He was a detective? JJ felt something shift inside his brain. Something was weird about this trip, and it wasn't anything to do with ghosts. JJ smelled a secret, if that was possible.

Detective Walker said, "That's correct. Penny is my granddaughter. We'll share a room."

"Very well." The butler sniffed. He stepped aside. "You can bring your luggage in and I will point you to the parlor—or perhaps you would consider it a den."

JJ was never quite sure what a den was. A sitting room? A place where you kept your lions?

His mom, the detective, and the butler went inside. But JJ was still taking in the Barclay Hotel. He couldn't believe his luck.

Penny saw a black cat in one of the upstairs windows. But when she blinked, it was gone.

Before she could tell JJ, another girl who looked to be about their age came running out onto the porch. "Here you guys are! Thank goodness. I thought this weekend was going to be a total drag."

Penny pushed her glasses up the bridge of her nose and frowned.

JJ blinked. "Who are you?"

"I'm Emma. And we're all going to be friends."

SOME PEOPLE LOVE to be on a team (like a Battle of the Books team, for example), working together, high-fiving each other, and all of that. Others like to work by themselves, in a little corner, preferably with a pencil and a notebook. In quiet. Penny and JJ were both more of the loner variety.

But Emma was clearly the team type. Her grin was so big that you could see her bright braces *and* the blue elastic bands on the sides. Her plaid shirt hung loose over a faded T-shirt with a band picture on it—the Black Eyed Peas. JJ almost asked her about it, but then he remembered that he wasn't at the Barclay to make friends. He was on a mission to ghost hunt.

"And here I was thinking this weekend was going to be boring!" said Emma.

"There aren't any other kids here?" JJ asked.

"Nope." Emma shook her head. "We're just waiting on some lady named Finella, Fibella . . . something. The guests are all adults." She made a face and crossed her eyes. "You see why I thought this weekend would be boring?"

A tall man wearing a cowboy hat lingered on the porch. He looked like he didn't want to go inside. And JJ saw Ms. Chelsea, the town librarian. He did his best to avoid looking at her—she'd probably remind him of the overdue Book Club books that were somewhere under his bed. But JJ really didn't have to worry. Ms. Chelsea was too busy rushing inside, her blonde hair whipping behind her. She was carrying a large round bag.

"We should go inside," Emma said. "There's a cocktail party in half an hour. I heard there's going to be a *big* announcement." She leaned in close to JJ and Penny. Emma smelled like cookies. Or cake, maybe—no, it was frosting. She whispered, "Knowing Mr. Barclay, I think I have an idea what the announcement is."

"What?" Penny was curious.

Emma made a motion across her lips, like she was zipping them. "It's a secret. I've sworn an oath. Well, my uncle did. He's the chef here." Emma was a straggler too. No invitation, but here for the fun anyway.

"You can tell me," JJ said, as they walked across the threshold, into the Barclay Hotel. It smelled like old books and wood polish. "Technically, I'm not invited, so the announcement isn't for me."

Emma thought about it, then shook her head. "Nope." And she walked backward with a silly grin on her face, until she turned a corner and just vanished down the hall. This girl was odd.

Penny looked toward the reception desk. Her grandpa was arguing with Mr. Clark (probably asking for that spa service), and JJ's mom looked like she was about ready to join in.

"Check out these masks," JJ called from the other side of the den.

Penny walked over to JJ, past the big arched windows

that gave you a bird's-eye view of the sky and the mountains, and the deep valley below. It was a little terrifying to Penny, who'd never been in the mountains.

But she was going to be brave, she reminded herself.

Penny focused her attention on the wall that JJ had pointed to. There were about a dozen shadow boxes, the kind of frames where you put stuff on display. Each one had a mask in it: some were ornamental with embellishments like feathers and gems. Others were plain, black or white.

"Are they theater masks?" JJ asked.

Penny nodded. "I think so. Mr. Barclay loves theater."

"How do you know that?" JJ asked. He peered into one of the shadow boxes.

Penny shrugged. "I read up on this place before we came. I like to do my research. You know, we should look at that book you have, *The History of the Barclay Hotel.* I think I saw a map in there."

JJ pulled the book from his backpack. They sat in the big chairs by the enormous stone fireplace.

Penny took the book and thumbed through the pages. She quickly found the map listed in the index, and opened the book. JJ was impressed. He might just want Penny on his ghost hunting team after all. Even if she was a skeptic. "Look, it's all right here."

JJ leaned closer. The hotel was enormous, that was obvious from the map. There was a Cupcake Shoppe (spelled old-fashioned like that), a carousel, a bowling alley, a pool—there was even a hedge maze outside. "Wow," he muttered.

"Yeah—fun, right?" Penny said.

But JJ's mind was on his ghost hunting. "That's a lot of ground to cover with my basic ghost hunting kit." He really wished he had those big suitcases with tripods and power cable reels now.

Penny said, "You'll have to show me all that stuff later. If I'm going to disprove that ghosts exist, I'll need to join you." She flipped the pages of the book again. "I saw something here, a few chapters back . . ."

JJ tried to keep up, but all those pages with tiny letters

made him dizzy. Thankfully, Penny didn't make him feel bad about not liking to read.

"Found it! 'The Ghosts of the Barclay Hotel'—see, there's a whole chapter." Penny took a minute to read the introduction.

JJ looked at the pictures. They were black-and-white, and pretty fuzzy. There was one of a really tall man in overalls. "That's Mr. Roberts," JJ said. It said so under the photo.

Penny nodded. "It says that the ghosts are bound to specific spaces."

JJ nodded too. "They can only go where they spent most of their time when they were alive. It's one of the rules of the supernatural world."

"What other rules are there?" Penny glanced at the reception desk. Her grandpa was now arguing even louder. Something to do with a facial.

"The ghosts can't talk to each other, is another one," JJ said. "And kids are more likely to see them."

"That's handy for us, I guess," Penny said. She smiled. "*If* I believed in ghosts."

JJ ignored her jab. "What else does the book say?"

Penny flipped a page. "It says here that at the Barclay Hotel, midnight is . . ." She paused.

"What?" JJ asked.

Penny looked up. "Midnight is the ghostly hour."

11

"**MIDNIGHT AT THE** *Barclay Hotel,*" Penny went on to read from the book, "*is when all spirits are drawn out and the grandfather clock plays 'Ode to Joy.'*"

Just then, the clock chimed, making both Penny and JJ jump.

They looked at the grandfather clock. JJ said, "That one?"

"I guess we'll find out at midnight," Penny said. "Spooky." She flipped the pages. "There's also a whole section about Mr. Barclay's family. Says here he has a daughter named Constance."

"Why don't we go check out the hotel instead of reading about it?" JJ said.

Penny nodded and closed the book.

JJ took the book from Penny, who was reluctant to let it go. She could have it as far as JJ was concerned, but his dad probably wouldn't agree. He'd given the book to JJ, after all.

Just then, Penny's grandpa walked over, looking grumpy. "There is no spa."

Penny said, "Oh, bummer. But there's a hot tub, right?"

"That hot tub better be good," Detective Walker grumbled.

"That's what I said," JJ's mom said. She handed JJ a room key. "I wonder what this welcome party is about. All they said was that there will be a big announcement. Do I really have to go?"

"Sounds ominous," Detective Walker said. "I guess we'll find out. And yes, I think you do."

The butler was motioning for them to come to the dining room. "You can check your rooms out later. Right through these doors, please."

"What about me? I'm just a kid, right? So I shouldn't

have to go," JJ said to his mom. "I think checking out the hotel would be a better use of my time. Don't you?"

"No wandering children," the butler said in a no-nonsense voice from behind them.

"You heard the man," his mom said, pointing in the direction of the dining room. "Maybe they'll have some hot cocoa for you."

Once inside the dining room, JJ locked eyes with the finger food. He suddenly realized how hungry he was—must be all that high altitude—so he started to fix himself a plate.

"Young man, get away from the hors d'oeuvres," Mr. Clark said as he swatted at JJ's hand.

"The what?" JJ said with a puzzled look on his face.

"First, the announcements. Then the food."

JJ sighed and moved closer to his mom. They all stood there, looking lost. JJ's mom kept checking her phone for no reason, and moving around the room to see if she got any reception.

Penny said behind him, "Your mom really likes her phone, huh?"

"It's because it's how she keeps up with her business," JJ said, slightly defensive. "She's the CEO of PB&JJ."

Now he had to give the usual speech, the one he always gave when people asked.

When he was a little toddler, JJ was a very picky eater. His mom realized he liked peanut butter and jelly sandwiches, so she became an expert at making them. But because she was worried JJ would get bored, she started adding fun stuff to the sandwiches, like marshmallow fluff, fried potatoes, and even carrots. JJ loved it, and so did everyone who ever came over. His mom decided to start a restaurant. It was so super successful, she added another restaurant, then another.

"And the rest is PB&JJ history," JJ said, finishing the story with the famous company line from the commercials.

Penny said, "There's a PB&JJ in my town. I *loooove* the PB and banana sandwich."

JJ liked Penny a little better already. "That is one of my favorites too. Maybe my mom can make them for us if the kitchen has the ingredients."

Before Penny could agree with this brilliant idea, two

women walked into the dining room: the librarian Ms. Chelsea and another young lady in a floral dress, wearing high heels that almost made her trip. That was actress Fiona Fleming. The cowboy followed close behind and sat at a table in the back, eyeing the pile of little sandwiches.

"Excuse me, everyone." Mr. Clark waited a moment. "If I can have your attention for this evening's announcement."

He let the silence echo around the room. Mr. Clark clearly liked a bit of drama.

"I'm pleased to welcome our esteemed guests to the Barclay Hotel for the weekend." He glanced at JJ and Penny. "Plus, a straggler or two, it seems."

JJ smiled. He didn't mind being called a straggler—it made the whole weekend seem more adventurous somehow.

Penny frowned. She didn't like how Mr. Clark made her feel like an annoying little kid.

Mr. Clark continued with his boring speech. "Most of you *invited* guests have had business with Mr. Barclay. Which is why each of you is here."

The room got so quiet when he paused, you could hear the guests' pulses quicken. Mr. Clark was milking this dramatic moment for all it was worth.

"These dealings were not always pleasant, or to your liking." Mr. Clark made a point of looking at every person in the room. "Which is why, exactly a week ago, one of you in this room killed Mr. Barclay. And this weekend, we will find out who the murderer is."

A KILLER? RIGHT here, in this room? JJ caught his mom turning the color of a tomato, and Jackie wasn't one to fluster easily. She was usually the one telling other people to troubleshoot stuff.

"Wow," Penny muttered as a grin spread across her face. "We're in a real-life murder mystery!"

Mr. Clark paced around the room with his hands clasped behind his back and continued, "A little-known fact about Mr. Barclay is that before he built the family fortune in real estate holdings, he invented a little board game called Catch a Criminal."

He paused for dramatic effect.

But before he could continue, JJ blurted out, "Oh, like Clue!"

"No, not at all like Clue," Mr. Clark snapped.

Clearly, this was a touchy subject.

"The game never became the hit he expected, but the original now lives in the library, if anyone is interested in playing."

Mr. Clark looked as if he expected at least one of the guests to jump at the chance to play this game . . . but no one seemed very interested. And how could you blame them? They had just been told that they were suspects in a murder. The premise hit a little too close to home at the moment.

Fiona cleared her throat and raised her hand, like she was in school. "Excuse me?"

"Ms. Fleming, you have a question." Mr. Clark even sounded like a teacher, all calm and patient.

Fiona paused, and glanced around the room to make sure everyone was paying attention to her. "Are *we* supposed to solve this mystery? Why aren't the police involved?"

"That's what I want to know," Buck Jones added.

"Please give me a chance to explain Mr. Barclay's intentions for this game," Mr. Clark said, slightly irritated. This conversation was getting away from him. "The police did a preliminary investigation and Mr. Barclay's physician attended as well. Both concluded that Mr. Barclay's death was caused by a heart attack. But I know it was really death by poison!"

There was a dramatic gasp, coming from the actress in residence, Ms. Fleming. "Murder. Poisoning means *murder*," she added, stating the obvious.

"Who said he was poisoned?" the detective countered.

"I requested that the police revisit this matter, so the medical examiner did an autopsy," Mr. Clark said. His face was sad. "It was indeed poison that killed Mr. Barclay."

"That's murder all right," Penny whispered, so only JJ could hear.

"Crime scene investigators have already been here at the hotel. Detectives will be coming on Monday to gather evidence and question witnesses," said Mr. Clark.

"However, Mr. Barclay was sure you—the four suspects and one detective—could solve the murder this weekend."

Ms. Chelsea asked, "How did Mr. Barclay even set all this up? I mean, he *is* dead."

Mr. Clark said, "Mr. Barclay knew he had enemies, and feared one of you might kill him. With his love for games, he decided to orchestrate one last game—from the grave, if you will. Upon his murder, he arranged for the invitations to go out and for me, his right-hand man, to ensure the game would move forward."

The room had gone eerily silent now. Murder was serious business.

Mr. Clark added, "Of course Mr. Barclay hoped he was wrong—no one wants to be murdered. But he had some serious quarrels with four of you invited guests."

JJ had hoped to talk to Mr. Barclay about the mansion's hauntings. Now that the man was dead, the whole weekend felt like it had a big fat dark cloud over it.

"Well, I am no killer," Ms. Chelsea said. "How do I clear my name?"

"That's what all suspects say," Ms. Fleming said, rolling her eyes with a snooty look on her face.

Mr. Clark ignored the actress and turned his attention back to Ms. Chelsea. "Play the game," he said with a mischievous expression. "There will be five players: Detective Frank Walker, Ms. Fiona Fleming, Mr. Buck Jones, Ms. Chelsea Griffin, and Mrs. Jackie Jacobson."

Next, Mr. Clark pointed to a table in the back, where leather-bound notebooks and pens were spread out. Five of each—one for each of the invited guests. "To clear your name, each of you must investigate the murder of Mr. Barclay. By the end of this weekend, I want to know who the real killer is."

All the guests stared at one another, a little dumbstruck. No one said a word.

Mr. Clark said, "Of course, one of you will not want the criminal to be caught."

"Because one of them is the murderer," Penny whispered to JJ.

That was clear to everyone.

Mr. Clark might as well have had ultrasonic hearing, and shot Penny some dagger eyes from across the room for stealing his thunder. He cleared his throat again. "Ladies and gentlemen, go catch a criminal."

TENSIONS RAN HIGH. There was some yelling and even cowboy-hat-throwing. Ms. Chelsea was the first to raise her voice, which was ironic because she spent much of her time shushing people at the library. You can guess who threw a cowboy hat.

Buck then quickly picked it up and grabbed a notebook from the table before storming off.

"I'm not playing," Detective Walker said, crossing his arms over his chest as if to emphasize his announcement. "I retired six months ago. I didn't come here to work."

Penny was so disappointed. Something exciting was finally happening, and now her grandpa didn't want to join in!

"No one will be forced to participate," Mr. Clark said. "But by the end of the weekend, we will have our murderer. Detective Walker, it's my understanding that you've solved every single case in your entire career. I believe it's why Mr. Barclay invited you. You are the best detective in the state of Colorado." Mr. Clark tried to hand Detective Walker a notebook.

"I'm retired," Detective Walker said firmly. He looked grumpy. "These sandwiches are hardly a five-course meal."

"It's still to come," Mr. Clark promised.

Detective Walker added, "And I wondered if you put me in room two seventeen on purpose."

Mr. Clark made an attempt to hide a smile, but did a terrible job.

"That's the most haunted room in the hotel!" JJ blurted out. He was a little peeved that he wasn't chosen to stay in that room. He would've appreciated it much more than this detective. His mom shot him a warning look that told him to stop talking.

Penny was more excited now. This was the perfect opportunity to debunk the Barclay Hotel's haunted reputation, since she was also staying in room 217.

"Young man, that's poppycock," Detective Walker said. "Ghosts aren't real."

Mr. Clark stepped in to challenge the detective. "Then the room shouldn't be a problem for you, should it?"

Detective Walker squinted, stepped back, and grumbled something.

While wrapping a few little sandwiches in a napkin, JJ's mom said to him, "I think we need to call this weekend off. I'm sorry, JJ, but this is madness."

"No one leaves," Mr. Clark bellowed from across the room. There was that ultrasonic hearing again. "At least, not until tomorrow." Mr. Clark tried to soften his tone and smiled. "The driver is off for the day, and besides, it's too dangerous to navigate the mountain roads at night."

You could hear a collective groan from all the guests in the room.

Fiona looked like she might cry as she left the dining hall.

JJ's mom held the notebook and turned to JJ. "I need to talk to my legal team—I'll go see if there's cell phone reception anywhere else in the hotel. See you at the room in a little while?"

"Sure, yeah," JJ said, his face falling slightly.

"Maybe we can check out the pool together," Jackie said, sensing his disappointment. "I hear there's a big slide."

Now that did sound really fun. JJ nodded. "Deal."

JJ's mom took the little sandwiches and rushed out the door.

After telling Penny to come upstairs as soon as possible, Detective Walker made his exit and went to room 217.

When Penny and JJ went out into the den, they found Emma practically bouncing up and down with excitement. "This is so awe-*soooome*!"

"What about this is awesome? Didn't you hear Mr. Barclay is dead?" JJ said.

Emma's excitement disappeared at the mention of Mr. Barclay. "I already knew about Mr. Barclay's death. I practically live here, remember? I'm going to miss Mr. Barclay very much." Emma blinked her tears away.

"Are you okay?" Penny asked.

Emma took a deep breath and brought her grin back. "Yeah, I'm fine. But we should solve this murder."

Penny said, "I agree with Emma. Let's do it!"

JJ thought about it all. If his mom got her way and they left tomorrow morning, his only chance to ghost hunt would be tonight. And with Mr. Barclay dead, there could be a new ghost to find. No offense to the deceased, of course. JJ was more determined than ever to get his equipment set up for the night. Maybe he could catch the ghost of Mr. Barclay and prove Penny wrong all at the same time.

JJ also thought of his mom, and how she was a suspect. He had to investigate this murder to clear her name. JJ turned his attention back to Emma and Penny.

"I have one condition. I want time to ghost hunt too."

Penny wanted to object to the existence of ghosts, but since JJ had just agreed to help them, she thought it might be better to keep quiet for now.

"We're like the three musketeers," Emma said.

Penny smiled. "Yes." She wouldn't admit it, but she was a little afraid—I mean, this *was* murder they were talking about. And if Mr. Clark was right, then there was a killer not too far away. Right here at the hotel.

"I told you two that we'd be great partners!" Emma said.

Penny shoved away her fear and said, "Stragglers have to stick together." She raised her hand to high-five Emma, but Penny only caught air.

Emma was already bolting down the hall.

After all, they had a murderer to catch. And not much time to do it.

"WE NEED A headquarters for our investigation." Emma paused to think for a second. "I know just the place." She darted off again, expecting the other two to follow.

The three kids went up the stairs, and then down the hall. They passed the room JJ and his mom were sharing on the way, and JJ wondered if she was in there. Was his mom involved in this murder—or worse: was she the murderer? It had to be a giant mistake.

"Do you think maybe Mr. Clark is wrong about Mr. Barclay's death being a murder?" he asked Penny. Emma was now up ahead, impatiently waiting for the two of them to catch up.

"Why would he lie?" Penny asked.

JJ didn't know how to answer that question. He just didn't want his mom to be a suspect.

Penny added, "It does seem like we're missing something, though. Like an important clue."

"We should figure out what clues there are," JJ said. He was eager to solve the mystery of Mr. Barclay's murder, to clear his mom's name, and to get to ghost hunting—that was the whole reason he was here, after all. He looked around, hoping to catch a ghost.

The lights flickered. "Dude," JJ whispered.

Before Penny could say anything else, the two kids heard Emma's voice from down the hall.

"This way!" she called.

Ghost hunting would have to wait. JJ sighed and joined Penny and Emma.

Emma opened a door, which led into what looked like another hotel room, only it wasn't. It was a small space, almost like a dressing room, with two giant wardrobes and a mirror. Emma grinned as she opened one of the wardrobes. "When I was little, I'd pretend I was going to Narnia. You know, like the book?"

The Lion, the Witch and the Wardrobe was on the Battle of the Books list, but JJ didn't want to admit that he'd never read the whole thing. He did, however, know she was talking about the wardrobe being a portal into a different world.

"I loved that book," Penny said.

JJ wondered if he was missing out, not reading. But it took him forever just to read the first few chapters.

Emma pushed the clothes aside and opened a small door. It led to another narrow hall, only the walls were bare this time.

The hall seemed to climb like a ramp before they reached another door. Emma opened the door, and they arrived in another sitting room.

Penny sat in one of the oversize chairs. It looked like it was going to swallow her whole, it was so giant.

Emma sat in another chair. "This room is right over the kitchen," she said. "Sometimes, I can hear dishes and silverware clanking as they hit the counter, and smell what my uncle is cooking up for Mr. Barclay." She blinked as if she was holding back emotions.

"You must miss Mr. Barclay," Penny said.

Emma nodded, looking sad.

JJ scanned the room. The part of him that wanted to ghost hunt started wondering if it was haunted. While Emma was talking to Penny, he rummaged through his backpack and pulled out his EMF detector.

"What's that?" Emma stepped in front of him. JJ jumped at the sound of Emma's voice. He hated it when people snuck up on him.

Before he could manage to get too irritated, JJ's attention was diverted to the EMF detector and its sudden continuous beeping. The detector was about the size of a cell phone, with a small screen and lights that arced around the bottom of the device. It was going crazy!

"It's an electromagnetic field detector—EMF. It shows you anything with an electromagnetic field, like wiring in an old house, or ghosts. And look!" He showed both Penny and Emma how the lights on the detector showed there was electromagnetic activity. Right over by the wall in front of them, sort of.

"Maybe this room is haunted," Emma said.

"Because that detector thing is bleeping?" Penny asked with a raised eyebrow.

"It's science, you know," JJ muttered.

"We need to focus on the murder investigation first," Penny said. "No ghost hunting."

Emma smiled. "So let's figure out who killed Mr. Barclay."

JJ put the EMF detector away and pulled out his log-book and pen; he looked at the crisp white paper. "I don't know about you guys, but I have no idea how to catch a murderer."

"Let's read more of *The History of the Barclay Hotel*," Penny suggested. "There might be more in there about Mr. Barclay, and motives to kill him and stuff."

"No," JJ said quickly. He was beginning to really hate that book.

"Fine. How about we use the game?" Penny suggested. She pointed to a box in the corner of the room.

"Mr. Barclay's Catch a Criminal?" JJ thought about that for a second. "Isn't that just made up?"

"But it's Mr. Barclay's game." Penny motioned around the room. "He set this whole thing up, and brought all the guests here to try to catch a murderer."

JJ said, "Okay, let's use the game, then." He blew off some dust and opened the box. It sounded like it was exhaling. "It looks brand-new!"

"Mr. Barclay produced five thousand copies but sold very few. He has a whole bunch in storage somewhere," Emma said.

JJ put the box lid aside and pulled out the game pieces. There was a board, character cards, and clue cards.

"It looks an awful lot like that Clue game," Penny said.

"I've played this game once before," Emma said. She spread the game components out on the dusty wood floor. "It's more like a murder mystery game. You have to take on parts as players, see? You're each acting out a part."

There were disguises in the box: a mustache, silly glasses, a necktie. JJ thought about all those masks in the den, and Mr. Barclay's love for the theater, and suddenly this game made total sense.

Emma continued, "Everyone has to play a part, and one of you is the killer. You're supposed to question each other to figure out who the murderer is."

Penny thought about the time that her parents hosted a murder mystery game at their house. She had so much fun, and this board game sounded the same.

JJ put on the silly glasses. "Honestly, I don't see how this helps us find Mr. Barclay's killer."

Penny pulled out a notepad. "We create character sheets, like these. Then we add clues—secrets we find out about the others—which will tell us whodunit."

"Who-whatsit?" JJ asked.

"Whodunit," Emma said, like JJ should know. "That's the killer, but you also call a mystery story that: a whodunit."

"All my favorite Agatha Christie novels are whodunits," Penny added. All serious mystery readers who practically live at the library, like Penny, know Agatha Christie.

JJ took off the silly glasses and put them back in the box.

Penny put the game's notepad back too. "I know what we need to do."

Emma and JJ looked at her.

Penny said, "My grandpa is—*was*—a detective, so I learned a few things from him. We need to interview our suspects, and find out three things."

Her two new friends looked at her in suspense.

"We need to find out who had motive, means, and opportunity."

PENNY FELT HERSELF getting nervous over being the center of attention, but she relaxed when she remembered that she really knew her stuff when it came to detective work. She'd watched her grandpa (when he was still a detective) because Penny secretly wanted to be a detective herself. Everyone just saw her as "Bookworm Penny," but she wanted to be more. Penny wanted to prove that she could be brave too.

This was a good start.

"Every murder mystery game has you interview characters to find out if they had motive—that's a reason to commit the crime," Penny said, feeling confident. "Then you look for means—that's if they had the tools to do it—and opportunity." She took a breath. "Opportunity is sort of obvious."

Emma and JJ were quiet, both impressed by how much Penny knew about investigating a murder.

"As a detective," Penny said, "once you figure out who had all three of those pieces of the puzzle, you've solved the mystery. Theoretically anyway. So, motive, means, and opportunity are the building blocks of an investigation." Penny knew she sounded like a grown-up, because her grandpa used to say the very same thing all the time.

"You make it sound so easy," Emma said.

Penny paused. "Don't be fooled. It's *very* hard."

Emma smiled. "Wow, Penny! You're a true detective. We're lucky to have you here."

Penny was a little shy when it came to receiving praise, but she smiled brightly. "I learned from my grandpa."

"Impressive," JJ muttered. He felt uneasy, given that his mom was one of the suspects. But that just meant he had to prove she *didn't* have the motive, means, and opportunity.

"So now what?" Emma was itching to move. You could tell she was excited to play this murder mystery game. She'd been bored as the only kid in this hotel for far too long.

"Well . . ." Penny looked at the Catch a Criminal game. "Now we play the game, just like Mr. Barclay intended. First thing we do is interview the four suspects."

JJ said, "I'll go talk to my mom."

He wasn't exactly impartial, and Penny tried to tell him that someone else should be doing that interview, but he was already headed toward the door.

"I'll question Fiona," Emma said.

Penny nodded. "I'll go find Ms. Chelsea, the librarian. Let's meet back here this evening, at nine," she added. "And that cowboy—what's his name?"

"Buck Jones." Emma had a great memory. "He seemed kinda shifty . . ." she said.

"I'll see if I can track him down too," Penny said. "We should start with motive. Who wanted Mr. Barclay dead, and why?"

PENNY WENT TO look for the librarian and the cowboy, and figured that the den might be the place to start. That seemed to be where people liked to hang out when they weren't in their rooms. As she came down the stairs, she heard someone talking and froze. She dashed behind a giant plant for cover.

"No, that's not at all what we agreed on." It was Mr. Clark, only he sounded different. He was less snooty, and his voice was deeper. Also, Mr. Clark, who had a very fancy English butler accent, now sounded more like a regular American person.

There was silence. Mr. Clark was on the phone.

"I need to know the specific time. Without it, we won't be able to determine time of death, or find the killer."

Penny felt a sense of discomfort.

Mr. Clark is only pretending to be British. But why?

Penny stayed in her hiding spot until she heard footsteps that indicated that Mr. Clark was walking away. Thank goodness. She didn't want to be caught eavesdropping.

Once she was sure Mr. Clark was gone, Penny entered the den and found it empty. No librarian, no cowboy, no guests at all. But while she was looking, Penny kept thinking of Mr. Clark, and how odd it was that he sounded like a different man when he was on the phone.

She couldn't help but wonder who Mr. Clark really was. And what was he hiding?

JJ PUT HIS key in the lock and entered his hotel room. He thought about what motive his mom might have to kill Mr. Barclay. Certainly, she didn't have any motive, JJ thought. She made PB&Js for a living, for goodness' sake! Murderers weren't sandwich artists, right?

JJ wanted to ask her, but his mom wasn't in their room. And it wasn't like he could send her a text, given that there was no cell phone reception and all. Anyway, what would he say? "Hey, Mom, did you kill Mr. Barclay?" Investigating your own mom for murder was complicated.

There were three sticky notes on the mirror, written in his mom's handwriting:

MOM

JAM

BATH

For most people, these three notes wouldn't mean anything. But JJ and his mom had their own language. Those three sticky notes were the clues JJ needed to find his mom.

Mrs. Jacobson's suitcase was open on the big bed, and her clothes had been moved around. Like she'd been searching for something.

Still, JJ didn't get it. The bathroom door was open, so she wasn't in the bathtub. He stopped to think for another moment.

Mom, jam, bath . . . Jam could be like jamming, as in music, but that made no sense . . . Maybe his mom was *in* a jam. Like being a murder suspect!

BATH wasn't an *actual* bath.

Those three words were part of his sight word list— somewhere in third grade, JJ thought.

His mom was in the hot tub. Hot tubs are like catnip

to adults, JJ knew. Especially adults who were stressed out, like his mom. Adults who were in a JAM.

He smiled, folded the sticky notes, and put them in his backpack. Of course, JJ was a smidge optimistic in his belief in his mom's innocence. Mr. Barclay clearly thought she was a suspect. That was why JJ's mom had been invited, just like the other suspects.

But JJ was biased. This was his mom, after all. She helped him with his homework, and often brought new PB&JJ sandwiches for him to try. She was nice to his friends, and always let anyone stay for dinner (even when it was the whole Book Club). A mom like that couldn't be a murderer.

JJ closed the door to their room and then locked up. He walked down the hall and stopped right past room 217.

What if he could get some ghost hunting in? Maybe just a little bit? He had that bet with Penny, and his plan was to do as much ghost hunting as possible—and what better place to start than the most haunted room in the hotel, right? Maybe Detective Walker would let him in.

JJ knocked, and waited. He even tried to use his key to pick the lock on the door, but it didn't work. Bummer. Maybe he could get Penny to let him in later, but then he'd have to listen to her try to disprove the existence of ghosts.

JJ decided this last option might be his only one. And Penny *was* a really good investigator—that could come in handy when ghost hunting.

When he got to the other end of the hall, he hit the call button for the elevator. He waited a full minute before the doors opened. Once he had gotten in, just as the doors began to close, a hand stuck inside.

"Hold up!" Penny called. She got on the elevator and gave JJ a quick smile.

"Where are you going?" JJ asked her as the doors closed.

"I'm looking for Ms. Chelsea. I think she might be bowling," Penny said.

JJ said, "I'm trying to find my mom. She's in the hot tub."

He pressed the button for the basement, knowing that was where the bowling alley was too. The elevator buttons were antique looking, faded with copper trim and dim light inside. There were mirrors lining the elevator walls.

Strange retro disco music was playing in the elevator, probably Mr. Barclay's favorite.

When the elevator was almost at the basement level, there was a giant *CLANK!* sound. The elevator and the disco music stopped. The lights flickered, then went off.

Penny made a squeaking noise, like a mouse. JJ sucked in his breath.

The elevator went pitch-dark.

WHILE JJ AND Penny were getting stuck in an elevator, Emma was off to look for actress Fiona Fleming, to find out why she might have wanted to kill Mr. Barclay.

Emma was the determined type—or at least that's what her dad used to say to her all the time. And look at her now! She was about to interview her first suspect—how exciting . . .

It didn't occur to Emma that she might be in mortal danger. Ms. Fleming was a murder suspect, after all.

Emma knew Fiona Fleming had to be in the theater—it was the logical place for an actress to be, right? Sure enough, the double doors to the theater were cracked open.

Emma slipped inside and could already hear Fiona

Fleming talking. She was in the center of the stage, sitting on the floor. She was laying out cards, and there was a candle lit across from her. The space was dark, but Emma could see the colors on the cards. They were tarot cards.

Was Fiona summoning spirits? Maybe Mr. Barclay's spirit?

The irony of this was that Mr. Barclay's ghost could easily point the finger at the killer.

Emma walked toward the stage, and Fiona squinted in the near dark to see. "Who is there?"

"I'm Emma. I'm the chef's niece."

The actress blinked, glanced down at her tarot cards, and then looked up at Emma like she'd just realized something. "Ah, yes. Welcome."

Emma stopped at the stage. "What are you doing?"

Fiona looked at the cards again. "I am summoning the spirits. In addition to my acting pursuits, I'm also a spiritual advisor."

Emma decided to get straight to the point. She said,

"I was wondering why Mr. Clark said you were a suspect."

Fiona looked away. "Oh, he is sadly mistaken. Mr. Barclay and I got along swimmingly—we're kindred spirits, lovers of all things theater," she mused.

"You seem far too nice to be a killer," Emma said, to get Fiona to like her. She sat down in one of the front-row seats. Like most kids, she knew that flattery could get you anywhere. "I think I've been to one of your plays once."

"Really?" Fiona perked up. "Which one?"

"The one in town, at the theater," Emma fibbed. "I can't remember the title . . ."

Fiona nodded, filling in where Emma couldn't. "Maybe *The Mousetrap*? It's such a great play, written by Agatha Christie herself, a brilliant mystery. But obviously not as good as *my* script." Fiona sure had a high opinion of herself.

Emma smiled. "You and Mr. Barclay both loved the theater. I can't see how you could have the motive to kill Mr. Barclay."

"Oh, and I don't," Fiona said. She moved toward the

edge of the stage, in front of Emma. "Well, I guess *technically* I have a motive."

Emma was dumbstruck. Was Fiona about to confess? Would it really be that easy?

"But I didn't do it!" Fiona added quickly.

Bummer, Emma thought. "What is your motive, then?"

Fiona hesitated, and rubbed her hands. "Mr. Barclay loves a good murder mystery. He invented the game Catch a Criminal—and that's basically just a murder mystery game in a box."

That's exactly what I said, Emma thought.

Fiona sighed. "I wrote the script for a murder mystery game, to be played right here in the Barclay Hotel. It was going to be a grand attraction, something that would make people come to the hotel, book a room, and stay. It was great! I based it on that Catch a Criminal game and everything."

Emma did think that sounded pretty fun.

"What went wrong?"

"I worked hard on it, and he seemed excited to bring it to the Barclay Hotel," Fiona said. "Then suddenly he changed his mind and said he'd have to think about it."

Emma saw where this was going. "Mr. Barclay said no."

Fiona nodded but hesitated before she kept going. "Without this deal with Mr. Barclay, I would go bankrupt and have to shut my theater down. It really was vital to me that Mr. Barclay buy my script, and that I would get to perform here at the Barclay Hotel."

"When did he tell you all this?" Emma asked.

"I was here Friday, for a meeting. Around ten o'clock in the morning."

Emma nodded, computing what she'd just heard. Not only did Fiona Fleming have a motive, she had opportunity too—she was here on Friday.

Fiona's eyes were tearful. "I swear, I didn't kill Mr. Barclay!"

But would anyone believe her? All suspects say that.

BACK IN THE elevator, JJ and Penny were falling to their death . . .

Okay, maybe that's a little overdramatic since the elevator had stopped. Both kids were still very much alive, thank goodness.

The elevator was quiet. Some kind of red emergency light had come on, so at least it wasn't pitch-black anymore. But the red glow made the whole thing extra scary.

JJ tried his flashlight, but the batteries were dead.

Penny felt her heart race—she hated small spaces—and had to focus on her breathing, to force herself to calm down. It was just a broken elevator. Someone had to find them eventually, right? Surely her grandpa or JJ's mom would miss them. How long could the grown-ups really sit in a hot tub before they started pruning?

"Is there an emergency button?" Penny asked.

JJ looked at the panel. There was one button, giant and red, and he pushed it. Nothing happened. And like anyone who's looking at a red button, JJ decided to push it a few more times, for good measure.

Penny hit the button too. "Shouldn't it light up or something like that?"

"Hello!" JJ called. But the elevator stayed completely silent.

Dead silent.

"What if it's the killer, trapping us here?" Penny asked JJ, like he knew.

"It's just an old elevator," JJ tried to say with confidence. He was worried too, but didn't want to admit it. It sure seemed like someone was determined to stop them from investigating the murder of Mr. Barclay.

But why?

"Helloooooo!" Penny called, her voice panicked. "Is it getting stuffy in here?"

"It's probably better if we don't freak out," JJ said. But it *was* getting warmer. Could they run out of air? He hit the red button a few more times, for no other reason than that it was the only thing to do.

And suddenly there was a buzzing sound.

Startled, Penny jumped onto JJ's back. "Aaaaghhh!"

"Whoa, are you okay?" JJ asked over his shoulder.

"No. Yes." Penny climbed down, embarrassed for being startled so easily. She had to be brave. She noticed an electronic pad. It had a grid with nine squares. "What's that?"

"I don't know. Maybe we should hit the squares," JJ said. It was the first thing he thought of, and why not?

Penny stopped him. "I think this might be a game. Mr. Barclay built all this entertainment into the hotel for his sick daughter."

"How do you know that?" JJ asked.

"I read it online before we came here." Penny studied the pad with the nine squares. "It looks like tic-tac-toe."

"Maybe if we play, it will let us out of the elevator," JJ said.

Sure, tic-tac-toe *looks* easy. But it's a lot harder to win than it seems.

"Do you know how to beat the game?" Penny asked JJ.

JJ said, "It's been a long time since I played . . . I think if you start, you have the advantage." The air was getting stuffier by the second. They had to hurry.

After a moment of hesitation, Penny touched the center square. A circle marked the spot.

The top right showed an X. Penny responded with a circle in the bottom corner. The game continued but ended in a tie. And then the board cleared. This time JJ played, but the game just kept coming to a stalemate. No one was winning. And what was worse, the computer seemed to get frustrated, speeding up its answers, the pad feeling warm to the touch.

It was an angry computer—and a pretty scary one at that.

This was when JJ had an idea, the kind that comes from strategic thinking. JJ might not be the best at reading, but he was a whiz at seeing the big picture.

He stopped and took a step back. Maybe the only way to beat the game (and the elevator) was to walk away.

"I quit," JJ said to the elevator ceiling (he wasn't sure why he looked there, but he imagined some puppet master up above laughing hysterically). "There is no way to win."

The screen started filling in Xs all over the tic-tac-toe grid, over and over and over. It was freaking JJ and Penny out.

"You made the game mad," Penny whispered to JJ.

The delirious pace kept going and going and going, until there was a low hissing sound. Smoke came from the screen, and it went black.

Silence filled the space.

Penny held her breath. JJ wondered how much longer they'd be stuck there.

There was a faint haze surrounding them. JJ paused and waved his hand. For a second he thought it might be a haunting—a ghost!

But it turned out to be more like the haze from a fire.

Penny noticed it too. "There's smoke!"

And it was getting harder to breathe. JJ coughed. The smoke was getting thicker. Had he made the game so mad, it decided to kill them?!

There was another loud *CLANK.*

Penny yelled, "Help!"

TURNED OUT THAT the *CLANK* was good news: the elevator was back in business. It took a moment, but then the lights came on and it moved. The smoke was sucked out through a vent.

First the elevator went up to the second floor, and then it came back down to the basement level.

The doors opened. There stood Mr. Clark and JJ's mom, looking worried.

"JJ!" she called. "I've been trying to find you. I even enlisted Mr. Clark here. What happened?"

He wasn't going to be a hero, not anymore. JJ ran out, fumbling his backpack. A paper fell out, and Penny picked it up. She was about to give it to him, but he was off to hug his mom.

Penny pocketed the paper to give to JJ later.

Penny and JJ told them about the elevator getting stuck, and then the tic-tac-toe game popping up.

Penny said, "You saved us, JJ. You realized we had to quit to beat the game."

Mr. Clark nodded approvingly. "Very clever." But then he frowned. "That game function is supposed to be shut off. Mr. Barclay installed it for his daughter," he said. "She loved tic-tac-toe. It was a secret game that would appear if you hit that red button ten times."

"*Ten* times?" JJ's mom asked.

Mr. Clark glanced at JJ and Penny. "You really hit the red button *that* many times?"

JJ and Penny both shrugged.

Penny said, "It was an emergency, Mr. Clark. The elevator was stuck. We thought you might get an alarm or something, and you'd come to get us out."

JJ added, "But the thing went crazy and got mad when we didn't continue playing."

His mom said, "It's an old hotel, JJ. Maybe the computer just broke."

Or maybe it was the hotel being haunted. Maybe it was the murderer. Why was it that adults always tried to explain things away?

Mr. Clark inspected the inside of the elevator. "Hmmm," he mumbled. "That's peculiar."

"What?" Penny asked.

"Mr. Barclay shut the game off." Mr. Clark looked very serious. "Someone sabotaged that elevator. They messed with the wires and activated the game."

"On purpose?" JJ asked.

"It seems so." Mr. Clark waited for the elevator doors to close. There was a hum that told them the car was going up.

Mr. Clark turned to walk back to the pool. "I must convince Detective Walker to get involved."

"I'm going to the bowling alley, to find Ms. Chelsea," Penny said to JJ. And she was off, before JJ could talk to her about this strange elevator business.

Jackie turned to JJ. "Let's take the stairs."

As they walked up the stairs, JJ worked up the courage to ask his mom what he came to find out. "Why did Mr. Barclay think you wanted him dead?"

JJ's mom stopped for a moment. She sighed and turned to JJ before she started walking again. "I think it's time I told you the truth."

They had reached their floor and were walking down the hall toward their room. "Mr. Barclay actually had a lot of money invested in PB&JJ," his mom said.

She unlocked the hotel room door. "When I came here for a meeting on Friday morning, Mr. Barclay threatened to make me pay back the entire loan he gave me to start the company. That would be really bad— PB&JJ might go under without his investment."

"Wait—you were here at the hotel on the same day that Mr. Barclay died?" JJ felt a sick, twisty feeling in his gut.

"Yes." JJ's mom sat down on the bed. "The truth is, Mr. Barclay wasn't wrong. I had motive to kill him, and I was here at the hotel that Friday. So I am a suspect."

THIS WAS NOT going at all according to JJ's plan. His mom had motive *and* opportunity—she was even there the day Mr. Barclay died!

"Of course, I didn't actually kill Mr. Barclay," JJ's mom added. "At the time of his death I was on my way home, on a conference call."

"Of course you didn't kill Mr. Barclay," JJ said with a nervous laugh. Because he remembered what Penny had said about motive, means, and opportunity. To any detective, his mom was still a suspect. Just because JJ knew his mom could never kill anyone didn't mean she was cleared.

"I'm sorry to get you mixed up in the murder investigation, JJ," his mom said.

"It's okay." JJ thought about the whopper of a secret he was keeping from her. He'd never shown her the letter he'd been carrying around in his backpack.

"Well, maybe you can at least get some of your ghost hunting in," his mom said with a smile. "I know that's the whole reason you wanted to come here."

"And to spend time with you," JJ said. Right about now, JJ felt really guilty about keeping that letter from his mom. It was hard to keep a secret around Jackie Jacobson. "But nighttime *is* good for ghost hunting."

"Just be careful. Oh, and JJ?" his mom said behind him.

"Yeah."

"Take the stairs."

MEANWHILE, PENNY WAS looking for Ms. Chelsea to find out her motive to kill Mr. Barclay, but the librarian was nowhere to be found. She wasn't in the bowling alley, the carousel room, the Cupcake Shoppe (which made Penny hungry), or the den. After running all over the hotel, Penny paused and asked herself:

Where would a librarian go, if she were visiting the Barclay Hotel . . . ?

The answer was suddenly so obvious that Penny felt foolish for not thinking of it earlier. She opened the heavy wooden doors and went inside the library. Penny stood amongst the bookcases lining the walls. The library smelled like old books and polished wood, and the upper level (reachable only by a spiral staircase), expanded as far as her eyes could see. This was Penny's favorite place to be—she felt at home in the library.

She took it all in and let out a sigh of delight. This had to be what heaven was like.

It was so quiet. This was the kind of silence that Penny loved when she was reading—there was nothing like being alone with a book, and getting lost in a story.

But when Penny returned her attention to the task at hand, she realized that Ms. Chelsea wasn't in the library.

"Ms. Chelsea?" she called, even though she was pretty sure no one would respond. "Hello . . . ?"

She looked up to see a black shape dart away. It looked like a cat. Penny loved animals, and hoped she'd be able to catch up to it.

Penny went up the staircase. Her footsteps were loud, echoing off the walls and the huge window that over-looked the valley. This place was amazing. She wished she'd brought her phone now, to take pictures for her friends at home.

Penny ran her fingers along the book spines, smiling.

She was busy getting lost amongst the books again when she heard a loud *THUMP!* She jumped, then saw that deeper into the library stacks, there was a big book on the floor. Penny walked over and picked it up, although she recognized the book by the picture of the hotel on the front.

The History of the Barclay Hotel

Obviously, someone *really* wanted her to read it. Maybe it was a ghost, she thought to herself. Whatever, or whoever, it was surely wanted her to take this book— borrow it, just for the weekend. Right?

"Penny?"

She walked over to the railing to see who was calling her name.

Her grandpa was waiting down on the main level of the library. "Where have you been?"

"Here," Penny said, which of course wasn't entirely true. She had been on that elevator, but she was afraid that if her grandpa knew that, he'd want to go home immediately. "I've just been here with the books."

And maybe the ghosts.

Penny smiled at her grandpa. "With the books," she repeated.

The detective gave her a funny look, as if he knew she was acting odd. But then he said, "Don't stay up too late," before turning around to leave. "We're leaving tomorrow. There are too many shenanigans going on here," he muttered on his way out.

Penny clutched her book and tried to shake the nagging sense that someone was watching her.

Seeing her grandpa reminded Penny of what she was supposed to do: find Ms. Chelsea and figure out what her motive was to kill Mr. Barclay.

Penny made her way down the spiral staircase. Before she left the library, she hesitated. Was this place really haunted?

But then she thought better of it.

"Poppycock," Penny whispered when she closed the heavy doors behind her.

There was no such thing as ghosts, and Penny would prove it.

IT WAS JUST past nine o'clock when JJ made his way to the secret room and found it dark. They had agreed to meet at nine, right?

"Hello?" His voice sounded extra loud in the deserted room. There was a shadow—there, in the corner of the room. Was it a ghost?

"Hey!" Emma jumped out from behind one of the chairs.

JJ stepped back. "You scared me." His heart was pounding. This girl was always a little . . . strange. Sometimes she was nowhere to be found, and other times she'd just show up out of nowhere. Emma certainly was like no other kid JJ knew. Maybe it was all this time at the hotel by herself.

Emma smiled. "Scaring you was the point." She planted her hands on her hips, looking fake mad. "You are late, mister."

"I was trapped in the elevator with Penny," JJ said. "We think someone did that to us on purpose."

Emma's face dropped. "Are you okay?"

JJ nodded. "I'm fine."

"Hey, guys, sorry I'm late." It was Penny.

"You missed me scaring JJ," Emma said with a grin.

"Get Penny next time," JJ added.

"No thanks," Penny said. "Did you talk to your mom, JJ?"

JJ hesitated, but he wasn't a good liar. "She was here that morning. And Mr. Barclay threatened to take back the money he'd invested in PB&JJ, so I guess that gives her motive as well. But I know she didn't do it!"

"Of course not. She's your mom." Penny opened her notebook to write things down. "So, I tried to find Ms.

Chelsea, but she must be hiding in her room." Penny couldn't really blame Ms. Chelsea. If Penny was a suspect in a murder, she might want to hide too.

"Bummer," JJ said. "We really need to figure out her motive."

Emma's face lit up. "Ms. Chelsea is the librarian, right? I remember hearing Mr. Barclay talking about giving a grant to a library once. But it was a while ago. I wonder if something happened to the grant recently."

"That would be a strong motive," JJ said. "Ms. Chelsea loves her job."

Penny asked Emma, "Did you get anywhere with Fiona Fleming?"

"She has a motive—she wrote a murder mystery script for the hotel, but Mr. Barclay decided not to buy it. And she was here the morning he died."

JJ felt relieved. His mom wasn't the only one with motive and opportunity.

Penny said, "Now we just need to know about the cowboy. I couldn't find him either. This hotel is enormous."

Emma walked around the room. "I wish we had one

of those whiteboards, the kind they have on police TV shows."

"Maybe tomorrow we can chase one down." JJ fake yawned. "I think I'm going to get some sleep."

Emma studied him, like she didn't believe what he was saying. And Penny did too. Clearly JJ was a bad liar . . .

But then Penny closed her notebook. "Okay, I guess. Some people have early bedtimes."

"Exactly." JJ let out a small sigh of relief that no one questioned him and walked toward the door. JJ was fibbing, of course, but he had good reason to want to wrap things up quickly.

"I just hope we get to close the case," Emma said behind him. "Your mom said you guys are leaving in the morning, remember?"

JJ did remember that now. But he wasn't sure he was cut out for this police work. All he wanted to do was roam around the Barclay Hotel and catch a ghost, instead of a criminal.

"We're only just getting started on our investigation,"

Penny mused as she opened her notebook again. "Maybe we can start early?"

"Sure," JJ said. He really did want to clear his mom's name.

But there was the other reason he was here at the Barclay Hotel.

So even though JJ felt a pull, the call of the case, so to speak, he decided to put it all in the back of his mind for that night.

It was ghost hunting time.

THE HOTEL WAS quiet when JJ made his way down-stairs. He had that big fat book about the history of the hotel in his backpack (it was heavy).

JJ kind of regretted not bringing Emma along. She probably would've known stuff about the passages and rooms, and about Mr. Barclay, that JJ didn't. But she was also loud. And when you're ghost hunting, it has to be quiet.

And Penny was too much of a skeptic. JJ was afraid she'd just make fun of him the whole time. He reasoned that a solo expedition was the best way to go.

The library took his breath away. Sure, he'd seen it in the books and photos they compiled on *Ghost Catchers*, but in person it was a whole different experience. There were shelves on not just one but two levels. JJ couldn't wait to use the spiral staircase to reach level two.

There were reports that guests smelled floral perfume here at times. JJ sniffed, but he didn't get a whiff of anything other than old books.

JJ set up his camera on the second level. It was pretty dark but not entirely, because of a large south-facing window. Wait—was that a ghost?

He jumped. "Aaaarghhh!" JJ called.

But it was just his own reflection in the glass. A rookie mistake—he had to focus. All this hunting for a murderer was putting him off his game.

It was after ten o'clock, but that didn't mean random adults (or murder suspects!) weren't going to barge in on his ghost hunting session. He had to get a move on.

JJ pulled out his EMF detector. There was no reading (not yet anyway). He set it down on a bookshelf.

"I thought I might find you here," Penny called from downstairs.

JJ felt his heart sink. "If you're here to debunk my evidence, you're going to have to wait a minute, because I haven't even set up yet."

Penny climbed the winding staircase. "I'm not. You dropped something earlier. I'm here to give it back." She handed him the letter that had been in his backpack.

JJ froze. His big secret was out.

Penny looked flustered. "I read the letter. I'm sorry, I didn't mean to snoop."

JJ sat on the edge of the staircase. He opened the letter and read it again.

Dear Mr. and Mrs. Jacobson,

This letter is to request your presence at our principal's office, Friday at four p.m. Your son, JJ Jacobson, is currently failing both his English and his history class. We need to discuss further steps urgently.

Sincerely,
Principal Miller

"I didn't know what to do, so I hid the letter," JJ said softly.

Penny nodded, showing she understood. It was a pickle, to keep a secret from your parents. "And then the secret gets bigger and bigger, the longer you hide it."

"Yes," JJ said, looking at her. "You get it."

"What are you going to do?" Penny asked.

"No idea." JJ sighed. "I guess they'll find out eventually. I just wanted to come here this weekend and forget about it all for a while."

"I hide stuff too." Penny sat next to him. "Everyone thinks that all I want to do is read. That I'm afraid of everything."

"Why?" JJ asked.

"I went scuba diving with my parents and a tour group last year, and I had a panic attack." She sighed. "I'm afraid of a lot of stuff, so everyone now just leaves me in a corner with a stack of books."

"What *do* you want?" JJ asked.

Penny said in the smallest voice, "I want to be brave."

JJ nodded. He knew what it was like to want people

to see you a certain way. "You were really brave in the elevator."

"That was nothing." But maybe Penny was wrong there, we can agree with JJ. She was braver than she gave herself credit for. "And I want to be a detective like my grandpa."

"You'd be a great detective," JJ said while he folded the letter. He stuffed it deep inside his bag. "Maybe you can help me detect ghosts."

"Not that there will be any," Penny added with a sly grin. "So, show me what equipment you're using."

He hesitated for a second, but then figured he could use the help. "Okay. I've set up the infrared camera over there." He pointed to the edge of the balcony.

"That's pretty cool," Penny said. "What does it do?"

"It records several hours of data." JJ adjusted the angle, so it could cover most of the library. "And detects temperature fluctuations too."

"Cold spots," Penny said. "I read somewhere that it's supposed to get cold when a ghost shows up."

"Sometimes, yeah." JJ studied her face. "I thought you didn't believe in ghosts."

"I don't." Penny shrugged. "But reading about them is interesting."

JJ had to laugh at this very Penny-style logic. She was here, so maybe she could help. JJ opened his logbook to write down any anomalies—those are strange things that happen during the night. And as anyone knows, night-time is the perfect time for spooky stuff.

He pointed to the EMF detector. "Maybe you can hold the EMF detector."

"Sure." Secretly, Penny was having fun. This ghost hunting stuff was pretty exciting, especially when she considered that if the invitation to the Barclay Hotel hadn't come along, she'd probably be watching *Antiques Road-show* with her grandpa.

JJ turned on his voice recorder. "You can catch audio evidence if you ask the ghost questions. Sometimes when you play it back, you'll be able to hear a ghost's voice on the recordings." It was in a staticky way, like when you were tuning in to the radio but the station was out of range. Well, at least if the ghost was a talker.

"Okay," Penny whispered.

"Is there anyone with us tonight?" JJ asked. That's what they did on the show. His voice echoed off the tall ceiling. He felt nervous, like he did when he was taking a test at school.

Penny watched the EMF detector's lights move up. Was there a ghost . . . ?

JJ walked around and asked his question again.

He looked down over the banister. And he saw a shadow. Right there, by the door!

"Penny," he whispered. "Look!"

THE BLACK SHADOW zoomed away and flew behind a bookcase.

"It's a cat," Penny said flatly. "I saw it in the window when we arrived."

"Oh." JJ did his best to hide his disappointment. "I was so excited for a second." Of course, JJ didn't consider that animals could be ghosts too. Penny had, but she wasn't about to speak up. She was still determined to prove that ghosts didn't exist.

JJ went down and back up the spiral stairs. He remembered the old reports that Mrs. Barclay roamed the bookcases. JJ searched for her spirit. He expected to see some kind of white apparition, but no luck.

Penny followed along. "Are you here, Mrs. Barclay?" she asked. The EMF detector only showed one light— no ghostly activity there.

They kept walking between the bookcases.

Suddenly, there was a thump behind them that made Penny jump. Several books had fallen on the floor between two bookcases.

Macbeth

The Mousetrap

Midnight at the Barclay Hotel

"They're plays," Penny said. Now didn't seem like the best time for Penny to tell JJ that *The History of the Barclay Hotel* had fallen from a bookshelf earlier that day. "I think that one script was written by Fiona Fleming." It had landed on the page with the list of cast members. Penny glanced at it, but not for long.

JJ said, "Maybe the ghost knocked them down."

"Or the cat." Penny put the plays back on the shelf. Her EMF detector lit up, but only for a split second. She was hoping to prove that ghosts didn't exist. So no news was good news—or no ghost was good news, better yet.

"If anyone can hear me, we'd like to talk to you," JJ said. He waited. There was about two hours of recording time on his voice recorder. He still had an hour and a half of time left on it.

Suddenly, he heard a whistling sound. It was coming from behind him, in the stacks.

JJ froze. Penny heard it too. There it was again! And the EMF detector was lighting up like a Christmas tree.

"Was that a ghost?" he asked Penny. The late Mrs. Barclay could be roaming the library *right now*. And he'd have it on tape!

"Poppycock," Penny muttered.

"Look at the EMF detector," JJ whispered.

"Huh?" Penny was excited now too. It was hard not to get caught up in the fun of ghost hunting.

JJ held his breath, and slowly walked between the stacks, careful not to make a sound. Penny followed, fully expecting there to be a logical explanation for the sound.

There! More whistling—and louder this time. That had to mean they were getting closer . . .

JJ and Penny moved to the next shelf. And waited.

The whistling was practically by their ears now.

They both tiptoed, turned the corner, and—

"BOO!"

EMMA JUMPED OUT of nowhere, causing JJ to fall back and land on his rear end. Penny yelped and her glasses flew off. She held on to the EMF detector for dear life, but it was completely dead at this point. Not a single light.

Emma doubled over in loud laughter, which the other two found very annoying. "You should've seen your faces!"

JJ was mad now. "We're working here, you know," he said sternly as he stood back up. "We were gathering evidence, and you just ruined it." He sounded a lot like his dad did that time the dog accidentally knocked his Colosseum puzzle off the coffee table.

"Emma!" Penny picked up her glasses and rubbed the

lenses on her shirt. "You scared the bejeebies out of me."

"Well, I managed to get JJ earlier, so it's only fair that I scare you too." Emma's face turned more serious. "What are you two doing? Are you ghost hunting or something?"

JJ didn't feel like answering her. Plus, his heart was still going a gazillion beats a minute.

"Yes, we were." Penny smiled. "It's kind of fun." This whole ghost hunting thing was growing on her.

Emma said, looking around the library, "I practically live here, and I've never seen any ghosts." Emma knew she was fibbing a little. But she didn't want all this ghost hunting to distract them from the murder mystery.

JJ held his voice recorder. "I'm trying to get evidence."

"You know, we should really work on getting evidence that is related to *the murder*," Emma said.

She had a point.

"But what if the ghosts know who killed Mr. Barclay?" JJ argued.

"Then they would just tell us," Emma said, rolling her eyes.

"She's right," Penny said. "And I think this thing

is out of juice anyway." She handed JJ back his EMF detector.

He wanted to argue, but he knew Emma was right. His mom was being accused of murder, and until they found proof of her innocence, she was still a suspect. "Okay," JJ said. He clicked off his voice recorder. "Back to the murder investigation. So, what's next?"

Suddenly, there was a huge ruckus coming from the south end of the hotel. The kids heard a lot of yelling and wondered what it was about.

Emma started walking down the library stairs. "That sounds like a fight." She seemed entirely too excited about that.

The three kids headed in the direction of the yelling.

They ended up down the hall from the reception desk, where a set of double doors were wide open.

Emma stopped. "Hey, guys," she said, looking uncomfortable. "I'm not allowed to go inside Mr. Barclay's office."

"Why not?" Penny asked. The yelling continued, and she was dying to see what the fuss was all about.

"I'm just not allowed." Emma stepped back. "My uncle said so. I'll just meet up with you guys later, okay?"

And she took off.

JJ and Penny looked at each other and frowned. "She's weird," JJ said.

"But nice," Penny added. She felt like she was a little weird herself sometimes. Penny liked the idea she wasn't the only one who was different. "Let's see what's going on."

Mr. Clark stood in the doorway, hands on his hips. "Well, well, look at this."

JJ and Penny had to crane their necks to see what Mr. Clark was well-well-ing about. Inside the office, standing on either side of the big mahogany desk, were Ms. Chelsea and Buck. Both were waving flashlights. And both were (suspiciously, JJ thought) wearing sneakers, when the cowboy had been wearing boots earlier, and Ms. Chelsea loafers.

"I caught him trying to steal a map!" Ms. Chelsea yelled. She was pointing her flashlight at Buck, nearly blinding him because it was aimed straight at his face.

"Talk about the pot calling the kettle black," Buck

countered. "You were here before me, Ms. Chelsea, rifling through the papers on Mr. Barclay's desk."

JJ's mom came up behind him, wearing her pajamas with an oversize *PB&JJ: Because everything is better with peanut butter!* sweatshirt over them. "What's going on? I could hear them yelling all the way in my room."

"They caught each other breaking into Mr. Barclay's office," JJ whispered. He wasn't sure why he was whispering.

Probably because the librarian was there. It was a force of habit.

"Yes, both of them did indeed break in," Mr. Clark said loudly. "Now that we are all up to speed on the day's events—"

"Why?" JJ and Penny asked at the same time.

"Excuse me, I'll be the one asking the questions here," Mr. Clark interjected. He turned back to Ms. Chelsea and Buck. "Now, please explain why you broke in."

Everyone looked at the two burglars, waiting for an answer. There was silence while Ms. Chelsea and Buck tried to come up with a reason.

Breaking the silence, Ms. Chelsea and Buck both spoke at once.

"Well, he—"

"No, she—"

"Stop!" Mr. Clark yelled. "One at a time. You first, Ms. Chelsea."

She hesitated, then said, "I admit I broke into Mr. Barclay's office. But it was only to find something that was mine, I swear!"

"What was it?" JJ's mom asked for everyone.

Ms. Chelsea sighed, and turned off her flashlight. "Mr. Barclay had promised to renew the library grant, but the funding never came through. I came to find proof that he had approved the grant." Her eyes were welling up with tears now. Forget the crazy plan for a slide and an arcade. "The library depends on that money. Without it . . ." Her voice trailed off. "As of Monday, I'm out of a job," she whispered.

Everyone was silent.

Mr. Clark said, "Surely Mr. Barclay would have approved funding. He has every year."

"That's what I thought!" Ms. Chelsea said. "But then . . ." Her voice trailed off again.

"What?" JJ asked.

"When I called on the phone early last Friday morning, I was told that the grant had been canceled." When Ms. Chelsea looked up, the tears were streaming down her face.

"Who told you this?" Mr. Clark asked.

Ms. Chelsea looked confused. "*You* did, Mr. Clark."

25

"YOU TOLD ME there would be no more library grant, Mr. Clark," Ms. Chelsea said. "And then you hung up on me."

Behind JJ, someone gasped dramatically. All the ruckus had awoken actress Fiona Fleming, so she'd joined the crowded hall that led to Mr. Barclay's office. She gasped again, even more dramatically, just in case anyone missed the first one.

Mr. Clark looked confused. "There must be some sort of mistake. Maybe you spoke to a prankster or called the wrong number."

Ms. Chelsea shook her head. "No mistake. I came

here even after you hung up on me, Mr. Clark. I drove up on Friday morning to speak to Mr. Barclay in person. I know how much he loved books."

"He does—*did*—indeed," Mr. Clark mumbled. "This is certainly a mystery, Ms. Chelsea." Still confused, he turned his attention to the cowboy. "Now, how about you, Mr. Buck Jones. What excuse do you have for breaking into the office?"

Buck was startled that the attention was on him all of a sudden. He was happier when everyone looked at Ms. Chelsea. "Me?" He pointed his flashlight at the desk. Papers were strewn all about. "I was looking for a document. But it seems someone was here before me."

"Nice try blaming the librarian," Fiona said. "Why were you breaking in?"

"For a map. A little like this one." Buck pointed to the frame behind him. It was a map of the Barclay estate, spanning acres of Colorado Rocky Mountain land.

Mr. Clark said calmly, "You were hoping to buy the ranch you're working on from Mr. Barclay."

All eyes were on the butler.

Buck looked Mr. Clark in the eye. "How did you know, Mr. Clark?"

Mr. Clark replied coolly, "Mr. Barclay shared all his business dealings with me. Which is why I also would've known if he wasn't planning to renew the library grant." He darted his eyes toward Ms. Chelsea as he said this last bit before looking back at the cowboy and stroking his handlebar mustache. Penny noticed Mr. Clark was acting quite nervous. Like a man with a secret.

But no one else noticed his suspicious behavior.

"If you already knew, why did you bother to ask me why I was in the office?" Buck asked.

"Dramatic effect," Mr. Clark replied slyly.

Buck frowned before continuing. "I was doing great—I won the state cattle-wrangling award for best lasso!"

"Congratulations!" Fiona Fleming clapped excitedly.

"Impressive," Mr. Clark replied. "And presumably this came with a prize."

"A big prize—I won a ton of money and I had big plans for it," Buck continued. "I came to see Mr. Barclay on Friday, but he refused to sell me the ranch!"

"Mr. Barclay was not a very nice man," Ms. Chelsea said to Buck.

Buck nodded in agreement.

"Now, now," Mr. Clark said. "Let's not speak ill of the dead. Besides, Mr. Barclay was known for his generosity."

"Maybe you didn't really know Mr. Barclay," Ms. Chelsea said. She crossed her arms and looked smug. She seemed to have forgotten she was in trouble just five minutes ago.

"Very true, Ms. Chelsea," Buck said.

"And you still haven't explained how you don't remember talking to me on the morning of the murder, Mr. Clark," Ms. Chelsea said. She had sharp observation skills. Ms. Chelsea was a librarian, after all.

Mr. Clark nervously twisted the ends of his mustache.

"Maybe we should all get some rest," JJ's mom said. "Come on, JJ." She turned and walked back down the hall, and JJ knew he should follow. "And no more ghost hunting either."

"But I'll miss the midnight hour!" JJ called.

His mom gave him dagger eyes, which told him he was out of luck.

Penny said goodbye, after scribbling notes in her book. Clues for their murder mystery.

Everyone else went to bed, even Mr. Clark. They needed their shut-eye if they were going to solve a murder, after all. And things were about to get a lot more complicated . . .

THE BARCLAY HOTEL can be a confusing place, especially when you're on the hunt for a murderer. But by now JJ, Penny, and Emma had gathered a lot of information. And like any good detective trio, they'd been writing down all the clues they found and keeping track of the suspects, and they had figured out one important thing.

Mr. Barclay was right: everyone had a motive.

Fiona Fleming didn't get the acting job she worked so hard for.

JJ's mom could lose her beloved PB&JJ.

Buck Jones wasn't able to buy the ranch.

Ms. Chelsea lost her library funding.

In each of these four cases, Mr. Barclay had stood in the way of the suspects getting what they wanted. Plus, there was a new lead to investigate.

There was something off about Mr. Clark; he didn't appear to be who he said he was.

The clock would soon strike midnight, and the Barclay Hotel would once again go silent. Not everyone was sleeping, however, especially not those with motive to worry about. Those four suspects were probably tossing and turning in their plush beds, wondering how they were going to get out of this mess.

Emma couldn't sleep either. After she left JJ and Penny that evening, she went over the evidence again. And all that excitement over finally having friends at the hotel had her brain buzzing. So she decided to do what she always did when she couldn't sleep: take a stroll around the hotel.

It was just before midnight when Emma settled into one of the poufy chairs in the den. Emma loved how the chairs seemed to wrap around you all cozy.

She waited for the clock to chime—and sure enough,

there it was. (It also played Beethoven's "Ode to Joy" afterward, to add to the suspense). Emma wasn't afraid of ghosts, so she hummed along to the tune.

Emma relaxed on the chair and looked out the windows.

While the clock played its song, a lady in white floated down the stairs, Mr. Roberts walked in as if he'd been working in the garden, and a little kid with marbles ran up and down the den. But Emma missed the whole thing. Her eyes were on the windows—or more accurately, on the trees and the massive valley below.

It was quiet in the hotel, the kind of silence that in the Colorado Rockies invites nature to bring a little drama.

Because at exactly midnight, it began to snow.

PART III

THE MISSING PUZZLE PIECE

27

PENNY WAS BLISSFULLY unaware of the snow outside—in fact, you could say she was out cold. She fell asleep the minute her head hit the pillow. Not surprising if you consider that it was two hours later (and well past her bedtime) in Florida.

The little cot that the Barclay Hotel provided was pretty comfortable. Her grandpa was snoring up a storm, but somehow that sound was very reassuring to Penny. She was dreaming of opening up a detective agency, one where she would help kids solve mysteries. Wouldn't that be something?

Penny was far away in detective dreamland until she

began to feel a tickling at her toes. In her deep sleep, Penny's right foot had drifted off the bed and out into the open air. Someone (or something) thought it would be fun to tickle her feet.

"Huh!" Penny sat up in her bed.

Her grandpa made a snoring noise.

She looked around the room. There was no one there, and she couldn't find what her foot might have rubbed up against. Penny's first thought was that she'd imagined the whole thing.

She settled back into bed, covering up her foot. But then she realized that this was the perfect opportunity to draw out the ghost. If there even was a spirit there. After all, Penny didn't believe in any of that nonsense.

She carefully shifted her foot, sliding it out from under the covers, and closed her eyes.

Nothing happened. Penny was tired enough that she drifted off to sleep again. The covers were nice and fluffy, like wrapping yourself in a cloud . . .

There it was again! Penny was careful not to sit up

abruptly. She opened one eye. Something tickled her foot; she was sure of it.

She craned her neck. She was hoping to catch whoever or whatever it was that was tickling her foot, not scare it away.

It was dark, but Penny was sure she saw a round shape at the end of her bed. Right by her foot.

She craned her neck a little more this time. Until she felt the tickling again, and saw what (who?) was doing it.

It was a cat. The kitty was small and black, and it ran its narrow tail right along Penny's foot.

Penny laughed, covering her mouth so she wouldn't scare the cat away. Of course it wasn't a ghost! The hotel probably had a resident cat. "Here, kitty," she whispered.

The cat looked her way and froze. Like it was surprised it had been caught in the act of foot tickling.

Penny's grandpa snored, and mumbled, "There is no veal on my plate." He was probably dreaming of that five-course meal he was promised on the invitation (which had yet to be delivered).

The cat stirred, and bolted under Penny's bed. Penny sat up and leaned over so she could look under the rollaway bed she was sleeping on.

No kitty.

"Here, little one," she whispered. Not that she would wake up her grandpa by talking, what with all the heavy snoring. "Where are you?"

Penny got up and looked around the room. Behind the chair, under her grandpa's big antique bed. In the bathroom. She even looked inside the antique wardrobe, just in case the cat had found a way inside.

No kitty.

Penny sat on her bed. Where had this cat disappeared to? She turned, and there it was. Sitting on her bed. It let out a small meow.

"Hi, kitty." Slowly, carefully, Penny reached out to pet the cat. But she just managed to catch air.

The cat vanished just as quickly as it appeared.

Penny blinked, twice for good measure. But this cat was gone, poof!

"Poppycock," her grandpa muttered in his sleep.

Indeed. Penny sat for another moment before deciding to go back to sleep. For all she knew, this whole thing was a dream anyway.

Penny put her head on the pillow and pulled up the blanket. But she left her foot dangling out in the air. Just in case that cat decided to pay her another visit . . .

THE NEXT MORNING, breakfast at the Barclay Hotel was served in the dining room promptly at seven a.m. It was very difficult to ignore the smell of pancakes, eggs, and croissants wafting through the hotel.

JJ's mouth was practically watering when he and his mom made their way down the stairs. But no one was in the dining room. And judging from all the talking out in the den, something was going on outside.

JJ saw pretty quickly what all the fuss was about. Outside in the dim light of morning, the trees, mountains, and front lawn were covered in snow. Lots and lots of snow— at least a foot of the stuff. And it was still coming down in thick, fluffy flakes, the kind that could easily add another foot if it kept going.

"So much for leaving this place today," JJ's mom said next to him. She sighed. "I'm having some bacon and toast."

JJ was about to join his mom when Penny pulled him aside by the fireplace. "You see that snow? This means we're all trapped!"

JJ said, "I don't think anyone is too happy about that. Except maybe you and me."

Penny smiled. "We don't get snow in Florida. Do you think we could go sledding?"

"Not unless you want to freeze to death." JJ pointed to the swirling snow. "That's a full-on blizzard. On top of a mountain like this one, it's deadly."

"Bummer," Penny muttered. "It looks so cool, though."

JJ and Penny joined the detective and JJ's mom in the dining room.

When they reached the table, they heard the detective say, "It's a little on the cold side, if you want to know the truth."

"Breakfast?" his mom asked.

"No, no—the hot tub."

At another table was Buck (who looked very grumpy) and the librarian, who was reading Agatha Christie's *Murder on the Orient Express*.

"Everyone, may I have your attention, please?" Mr. Clark stood and cleared his throat. "As you all can see, there's a blizzard outside. I've been told that the roads are treacherous right now, and therefore no one will be able to leave today."

There was some grumbling, but the guests understood. Snow was snow—no way to make it stop.

"I do have some news to share," Mr. Clark said. "I received an update on Mr. Barclay's murder. I got a phone call a few minutes ago from the coroner's office in Denver." The coroner's office is where they take bodies to be examined. "They've concluded that Mr. Barclay ingested the poison between the hours of nine a.m. and eleven a.m. on Friday, March twenty-seventh." Mr. Clark paused for drama.

Detective Walker's interest was piqued. "What did he eat that was poisonous?"

Mr. Clark nodded, and paused again. "It was a treat. Mr. Barclay was poisoned with frosting. On a cupcake." Mr. Clark added, "The poison is apparently very easily obtainable. It's a simple blend of otherwise innocent chemicals, but when mixed together . . ." So, any of the suspects had the means to commit the crime: all they had to do was order the poison and bring it to the hotel.

The room seemed to be holding its breath.

Mr. Clark continued, "I know that Mr. Barclay had his tea and cupcake at exactly ten thirty on Friday morning. He was a man of routine and had it at the same time every morning."

Jackie said, "So the killer poisoned the frosting after the cupcake was on his plate, right before Mr. Barclay ate it?"

"That is correct," Mr. Clark conceded.

"Were there other cupcakes in the kitchen?" Detective Walker asked. "If so, did you have them tested?" He was a detective; he couldn't help himself. The detective felt a familiar fire in his chest, the kind that only came with a case to investigate.

Mr. Clark said, "Yes. None of the other cupcakes were poisoned."

"Who served the cupcake?" Buck asked in his deep voice.

Mr. Clark paused. "Have any of you figured out the motives for all the guests yet?"

"We have," Penny said. She immediately wished she'd kept her mouth shut, because everyone looked at her. It's a lot like raising your hand in class when you're so sure you know the answer, only to find you're the only kid with your palm in the air.

"It's true," JJ added. Penny felt better now that she was not alone.

"Very good," Mr. Clark said. "Although technically, you are stragglers. The four suspects should have been the ones playing the murder mystery game."

"A man is dead," Detective Walker said in an extra-stern voice. "This is not a *game*, Mr. Clark, whatever Mr. Barclay may have intended."

"Who served Mr. Barclay the poisoned cupcake?" Buck asked again.

Mr. Clark took a breath. "Mr. Barclay had his tea in the kitchen, along with that cupcake. His chef was the one who served him."

THE CHEF WAS Emma's uncle! JJ looked around for Emma to see how she'd reacted to this news, but he couldn't find her.

"That makes the chef a suspect too," Buck said, sitting back in his chair, looking smug.

Fiona added to the chorus. "Not just any suspect. If Mr. Barclay was poisoned by a cupcake's frosting, I would say that whoever made the cupcake is the *prime* suspect."

Everyone agreed that this was a logical conclusion to arrive at.

"So now we have five suspects?" JJ's mom asked, pointing out the obvious.

Fiona said, "I would say the chef is the *only* suspect."

There was murmuring, which turned into louder voices, protesting, and finger pointing.

Mr. Clark raised his hands. "Everyone, everyone."

Out of nowhere, Fiona stood up and clapped her hands twice. "Well, since I have everyone's attention, I'd like to announce that I'll be hosting my murder mystery game during dinner this evening. It's called *Midnight at the Barclay Hotel*. This way, I can show you all just how much fun it could be!"

Buck grumbled, "I think we're all fed up with murder mystery games, Ms. Fleming."

Everyone nodded.

Fiona's face dropped.

"Perhaps another time, Ms. Fleming," Mr. Clark said.

She sank back down into her seat, looking disappointed.

Mr. Clark said in closing, "To continue the game, you will need to interview each other as suspects. So ensure you all are available this afternoon."

"I NEED TO call home," JJ's mom said as they left the dining room.

"Hey, Mom?" JJ said. He looked down at his shoes. "I'm really sorry about all this."

Jackie looked surprised. "Unless you killed Mr. Barclay, this isn't your fault, JJ."

That wasn't exactly what he was referring to when he apologized. Lying to his mom about the letter from the principal was starting to eat away at him.

"Did you like the sticky notes?" she asked, smiling. This only made JJ feel worse, if that was possible.

"The tired MOM was in a JAM and decided to find the hot tub instead of a BATH," JJ said. It wasn't so awesome, but he did use all three words in a sentence.

His mom seemed to like it—she was JJ's mom, after all. "Nice one. I'll give you some new ones, later."

JJ nodded. He was a little old for the sticky notes at this point, but he didn't have the heart to tell his mom that he had long moved on from sight words. Sometimes, moms don't like to be reminded that their kids grow up.

"Maybe we can check out that pool later today," JJ's

mom said. "Right now, I have to go call your dad, and let him know what's going on over here."

A phone call. There was something about it that made JJ think it was a clue. He felt an idea forming in his head . . .

"You're awfully quiet. Are you okay, JJ?" his mom asked.

"Yeah, sure." He needed to think. And talk to Penny and Emma. "I'm going to do some more exploring of the hotel. See you at lunch?"

JJ's mom nodded and gave him a last hug.

JJ didn't waste any time making his way to the back of the room and down the secret passage, up the stairs to the secret room. Penny was there, poring over her notes.

Emma seemed relieved to see him. "Oh good, you're here. Penny just told me that my uncle is a suspect! We have to find a way to clear him."

JJ nodded. Penny made a face, like she was fearing the worst.

"He didn't kill Mr. Barclay!" Emma was nearly in tears.

"Okay, okay." JJ raised his hands in defense, then sat down in one of the old chairs. "Neither did my mom, you know."

Emma worked to compose herself. "I know. So, I guess it's up to us to prove that."

Penny said, "Let's see what we have so far. You have your notebook, JJ?" Once he handed it to Penny, she tore out five pages. "One piece of paper for each suspect. We have to add your uncle, Emma. If we want to rule him out as a suspect, we have to prove it."

"Okay," Emma relented. "You're right. Five suspects."

Penny made a drawing of each suspect on a different sheet of paper.

Buck Jones

Fiona Fleming

Jackie Jacobson

Ms. Chelsea

Chef Pierre

And then she added a sixth page called *extra clues.*

"These are great drawings, Penny," JJ said.

He went around the room, pinning the pages to the

wall, using the nails that were already there. Then he took one of the pads of sticky notes from his backpack. "For the clues," he said.

"Nice." Penny smiled, then her face got serious. She said, "Buck Jones. Motive."

Emma summed it up. "He wanted to buy the ranch, but Mr. Barclay wouldn't allow it."

JJ wrote down *ranch* on a sticky note, and put it under Buck Jones. Then he said, "But what would killing Mr. Barclay do to make that better?"

"Buck Jones was angry," Emma said, but she didn't sound convinced either.

JJ pointed to the next name. "The actress, Fiona Fleming. Another angry person?"

Penny said, "She wrote the murder mystery game script for Mr. Barclay. And then he turned her down."

JJ wrote *script* on a note under Fiona Fleming's name.

"Mr. Barclay is not a very nice guy, is he?" Penny asked no one in particular.

JJ nodded in agreement. "He was downright mean. He promised all these people things and then didn't deliver. What's weird is that he wasn't like that before."

Emma nodded. "Yeah, I think he was really nice, you know, normally." She scrunched up her face again as if she might start crying at the thought of him, but she looked away before the other two noticed anything.

JJ wrote *grant* on a sticky note for the library funding motive for Ms. Chelsea.

"Jackie Jacobson," Penny said softly. It was awkward, to say the least.

JJ sighed and looked at the wall. "Well, my mom had motive too. Mr. Barclay was going to make her pay back the loan she used to start PB&JJ." He put a *PB&JJ loan* note under her name. "I feel like there's an important clue I'm missing, something to do with the phones . . ."

"Like what?" Penny asked.

"I don't know yet." JJ chewed on the end of his pen.

"It'll come to you." Penny wanted to be encouraging. It couldn't be easy to have your mom be suspected of murder.

"The chef," JJ said, moving along on the suspect list.

"We don't know if my uncle had any motive," Emma said. "But since he's the chef, I would say he definitely had the opportunity. He served the cupcake." She sounded nervous.

"We should talk to him," Penny said.

"I can do it," Emma said a little too quickly.

Penny felt awkward but said, "An impartial person should question your uncle. Like me, or JJ."

"Sorry, Emma, but . . ." JJ said.

But Emma was already storming out of the room.

Penny sighed. She felt bad for Emma. She turned back to JJ and tried to figure out what to do next.

Then she remembered a clue. Penny got up and took a sticky note from JJ. She put *Mr. Clark has a secret.* "He is pretending to be British. I heard him, and he sounded American." She put the note under *extra clues*.

JJ looked at the wall. "Now what?" he asked Penny.

A deep voice went, "Now you find the person with opportunity."

THE DEEP VOICE belonged to Detective Walker. He strolled around the room and studied the sticky notes below each suspect.

"You did this?" he asked Penny.

Penny nodded. "With JJ and this girl Emma who lives here."

"Well done, kids."

Penny said, "Thanks. How did you find this room, Grandpa?"

Detective Walker smiled. "You're not the only one with detective skills, you know."

"You followed me?"

"Correct." The detective walked past the suspect list again and stopped by the *extra clues* page. "Do you have a pen?"

Penny nodded and handed the detective one.

Con man Gerrit Hofstra, Detective Walker wrote on a sticky note. Before JJ or Penny could ask, he said, "I spoke with my old partner last night. She mentioned that there were reports that this con man moved to the Aspen Springs area."

"You're investigating, Grandpa?" Penny asked with a smile.

Detective Walker grumbled, then said, "Just for this murder case. And maybe more from the sidelines. It sounds like I'm needed, so I'll come out of retirement for the weekend. But you kids seem to have most of it covered." The truth was that being a detective was like dodgeball: you were either in it or you weren't.

"Could this Gerrit guy have killed Mr. Barclay?" JJ asked. Another suspect could mean his mom was off the hook.

"We don't know if it's related," Detective Walker said. "But it's worth considering. This con man stole millions from rich people. Since Mr. Barclay was very wealthy . . ." Gerrit Hofstra could have killed Mr. Barclay and stolen his money.

"Is he in town? Did he come to the hotel?" Penny asked.

"I haven't seen him," the detective said. "Could be that this is a red herring—you know what that is?"

Penny nodded, since she'd read her share of mysteries. But JJ shook his head.

"A red herring is a false clue. Information that distracts you from who the real killer is," Detective Walker said. He walked along the evidence wall. "Something is off about this."

"Off?"

"There's a big puzzle piece missing." Detective Walker sighed.

"I thought the same thing," Penny said.

Detective Walker said, "When I investigate—or

investigated—a crime, and the evidence wasn't adding up, I would look back at who started it all."

Penny and JJ looked confused. This was a big crash course in detective work.

"The victim. Maybe the puzzle piece that's missing is Mr. Barclay himself."

DETECTIVE WALKER LEFT after telling Penny to check in with him at lunch. He was going for a morning dip in the pool.

"Let's first interview the chef," Penny said.

JJ agreed. "If Emma doesn't get to him first."

There were still breakfast smells wafting from the double doors that went into the commercial kitchen.

They found the chef cleaning a griddle. He looked angry.

"Hello?" JJ called. You don't want to scare someone who is working in the kitchen.

The chef looked up. "Yes?"

"I'm JJ. Mrs. Jacobson's son?"

"I'm Penny," Penny added.

The chef nodded. He seemed to remember that he was upset and continued scraping the large griddle. "Ah, *oui*. I'm Dominique Pierre, but everyone just calls me Chef Pierre," the chef said in a heavy French accent. "Did you get your breakfast?"

"It was great, thank you." JJ sat down at the small table on a wobbly old chair.

Penny did too. It wasn't until she sat that she realized that this was probably where Mr. Barclay sat and ate his cupcake, right before he died.

Penny was a little weirded out by this fact, so she sprang up again and decided to just stand for this interview.

Pierre noticed, and remembered too. "Oh, *mon dieu*. If only I had—" He stopped himself and shook his head. "*Non*. The police will come, of course, when the snow stops falling. But I cook until the end—that's what Mr. Barclay wanted."

"Were you here when Mr. Barclay . . . ?" Penny

couldn't get herself to say *was poisoned* or *kicked the bucket*. It was all a little too real to think that the man dropped dead right here, in this kitchen.

"I will not talk about it," Pierre said resolutely.

This was not going how they'd planned.

JJ turned to face Chef Pierre. Why didn't he want to talk about it? JJ could only think of one reason.

JJ said to the chef, "Is that because you have a secret to hide too?"

EMMA COULD FEEL herself getting more and more frustrated as she roamed the hotel. They weren't getting anywhere with any of the suspects, and now the chef was a suspect too! Mr. Clark wasn't any help either, and he'd been right here when Mr. Barclay died, right? Maybe it was time to look at the butler as a suspect.

Emma was already near Mr. Clark's room—might as well break in, she figured. Once you got started breaking and entering, one more time didn't really matter. (It does matter. Breaking and entering is technically a crime, just ask Detective Walker.)

Mr. Clark's room was tidy—almost *too* tidy. There were no clothes lying around, no personal photos. There was only his work schedule, pinned neatly to an otherwise empty bulletin board.

Then she looked in his closet and found . . . Well, it was difficult to describe. There were clothes, but not anything she'd seen Mr. Clark wear. Casual wear, even overalls, and Emma couldn't imagine Mr. Clark wearing any of those things. There were hats too, wigs . . .

Costumes. These were costumes.

Was Mr. Clark into theater? Emma couldn't remember, but then how well did anyone really know Mr. Clark?

Emma moved to his desk, and opened the top drawer.

There was a letter at the bottom of the drawer. Emma unfolded the paper.

I know who you are. You will pay.

It was signed *His Daughter.* A threat.

Who was this daughter, and why was she so angry with Mr. Clark?

NOW, SOMETHING TO know about JJ is that he was developing a radar for liars. Considering he was knee-deep in his own lying mess, it took a liar to spot a liar, one might say. And it also probably helped that Chef Pierre was a pretty terrible liar. One of the worst.

Chef Pierre finally sighed, and said, "Do you know how hard it is to be a chef at a fancy hotel? Everyone assumes that you're some sort of cooking genius. And I'm not! My skills are very limited."

"Breakfast was pretty awesome," JJ argued.

The chef sighed and dropped the spatula he'd been scraping the griddle with. "That's just bacon and eggs. Anyone can make that."

"And those little sandwiches yesterday—those were great," Penny added.

But the chef's face dropped. "I didn't make those. I only know how to make kids' food: pizza, hot dogs, and hamburgers. I love making food for kids—*c'est ma* . . . It's my passion."

"I'm not seeing the problem here," Penny said. "I love pizza and hamburgers!"

The chef said softly, "I bought the sandwiches from the deli in town."

"Oh." Penny tried to think of something nice to say, but she had nothing.

"And the cupcakes weren't mine either," Chef Pierre said. "I bought them from the cupcake shop in town. I wasn't even here when Mr. Barclay ate that cupcake. I was on my way into Aspen Springs, and on the phone the moment I got into cell phone range of the place to order. *C'est*—it's embarrassing."

Penny thought about that for a moment. "That means you didn't have opportunity to kill Mr. Barclay. We just need to prove it."

Chef Pierre nodded, but he looked sad.

"Wouldn't your phone records show that you were going into town?" JJ said, feeling a lightbulb go off inside his head. "There was no way you could be on a cell phone call if you were here, which means you have an alibi!" He was talking fast now because he was so happy.

This revelation could help his mom too! Because if the chef's alibi was a phone call, his mom would be cleared for the same reason: *she was on a conference call at the time of the murder.* The lack of cell phone reception at the hotel turned out to be the saving grace for both his mom and Chef Pierre.

Pretty smart thinking on JJ's part.

"*Oui*," Chef Pierre said, and gave him a half-happy, half-sad smile. He still looked devastated that his secret was out: he wasn't the chef everyone thought he was.

JJ turned to Penny. "I need to go find my mom. I might have found a way to clear her name."

"Let's go!"

The two left the confused chef, but JJ didn't have time to explain. He had a clue, and an important one . . .

33

EMMA PUT THE letter she had found in Mr. Clark's room in her pocket, locked up, and left. This letter had to be some sort of clue—her new friends JJ and Penny would be excited to see it.

She made her way to the library—her favorite place to think.

Her uncle couldn't possibly be the killer. Of course, Emma hadn't told JJ and Penny that he wasn't *actually* her uncle. Emma was just so afraid that if they found out her secret, they wouldn't want to be her friends anymore.

Emma sighed as she sat down on the library stairs. Not only was she being a terrible detective, she was being a pretty lousy friend too.

She had to do two things:

1. Prove the chef didn't poison Mr. Barclay.
2. Find JJ and Penny and apologize for running off.

She was about to stand up when she saw something in her peripheral vision. It was a round eye, watching her. A camera.

Emma got up and made her way to the second level of the library, where the camera was perched. It was set up in such a way that it had a sweeping view of the whole room.

She picked up the camera. Emma recognized what it was: an infrared camera, designed to detect fluctuations in temperature. Designed to catch ghosts.

It had to be JJ's. Either he had set it up and forgotten about it, or it was here to capture a ghost.

Emma tried to turn the camera on, but it was dead. Probably because it had been running all night. Or maybe because the spirits had drained the battery. At least that's what she'd seen on those ghost hunting TV shows: ghosts needed energy to appear, and they would draw it from whatever device they were near.

She should return the camera to JJ. It might have evidence on it, right?

Now, Emma was smart, kind, and respectful of others' property. But she was lonely. And a little afraid that JJ and Penny might leave right away, or get distracted from the investigation. They were supposed to be a team.

Emma was worried she'd lose her new friends.

She hesitated, but then gave the camera a good smack on the floor. The camera's case was cracked—that made it unusable, right? She felt bad, but she had good reason to break it. JJ would be back for the camera, so the best thing would be to just leave it where she found it.

Emma had to keep the secret of the Barclay Hotel. JJ and Penny didn't have to know.

She had to go find them, so they could prove her uncle innocent. And find the real killer.

JJ WAS SO excited that he took the stairs two at a time. He'd just cleared the chef's and his mom's name in one fell swoop! His mom was going to be so happy that he figured out she had an alibi, and JJ couldn't wait to tell her.

He hurried down the hall, and used his key to get into the room.

"I have good news," JJ started, as he walked through the door, but he quickly stopped when he saw the look on his mom's face.

She was sitting in the chair, looking as angry as he'd ever seen her. Her arms were crossed, and she had a dark expression on her face.

"You forgot to give me a letter," his mom said. Her voice was calm—the kind of calm that's only achieved when someone is actually really, really angry.

This was not good.

His mom went on, "I talked to your father this morning. He got a phone call from the school yesterday. Apparently, we missed a late-afternoon meeting with the principal and a few of your teachers."

JJ tried to swallow the lump that was in his throat, but it wouldn't go down.

"Thankfully, your father was already near the school for groceries, so he stopped shopping and met the principal. I'm sure you're *very* relieved to hear that, JJ." Her eyes were like dragon fire.

This was really, *really* bad.

JJ tried to think of something to say, but didn't have a comeback. His secret was out, and he felt terrible for lying all this time.

His mom sighed. "Why didn't you tell us about your grades?"

"I don't know," JJ said, his voice small as a mouse's.

"I'm sorry you're disappointed in me." He wanted to live up to his mom's expectations. And he really tried. But every time he had to read long passages or work on a test, he'd read the sentences but none of it made sense. Sometimes it didn't even stick after reading the passage three times.

He would often have to guess the answer. Whatever it took to get out of the classroom before the bell rang. And at home, he would pretend to be in his bedroom reading, but really, he was ghost hunting.

"Reading is so hard," JJ said. "I'm really trying, Mom. I think I'm just stupid."

"Oh, JJ." His mom got up from her chair and wrapped him in a big mom-hug.

Now, JJ was twelve, but these mom-hugs were just the thing he needed when the chips were down. No matter how old he got.

"Don't ever say you're stupid." She gave him a big smile. "You're so smart. Remember that time you won the robotics competition? That was a really complicated robot you built—the judges even said so."

JJ nodded, but he still felt like he'd let his mom down. "Now what? What am I going to do about my failing classes?"

His mom sighed. "We'll figure it out when we get home. At least now that your dad and I know the truth, we can help you, JJ."

That made a lot of sense.

His mom said, "If we were at home, I would ground you. But it turns out we're stuck here." She got up. "So you're grounded, JJ, at the Barclay Hotel. We'll figure out what your real punishment is tomorrow when we talk with your dad."

She went on, "Now I'm going to go meet Mr. Clark. And you had better stay here." She closed the door to their hotel room before JJ could come up with a reason to argue.

JJ exhaled. He hadn't realized he'd been holding his breath. Boy, was he in big trouble!

And he didn't get the chance to tell his mom that he found her an alibi. Next time he saw her, he'd tell her the good news.

JJ was sitting on the bed replaying the conversation with his mom in his head when he saw something white fly by, out of the corner of his eye. It was on the floor, near the door.

A sheet of paper. A note. Was this from his mother? She liked the yellow sticky notes, but she didn't usually write to JJ using regular paper. This note looked like it was written on the hotel stationery, the kind that was on the pad by the bed.

JJ picked the note up off the ground.

Meet me at the Barclay Carousel as soon as possible.

That was it? No name to say who sent it, or a date? JJ turned the paper over and read it again. He opened the door to see who might've left the note, but the hall was deserted.

Whoever left this note obviously needed to see him. What if it was Penny or Emma, with important information about their investigation?

He hesitated for a second, while thinking of his mom's orders to stay in their room, but then told himself he would be back before she even missed him. JJ grabbed his backpack, which didn't feel all that heavy anymore. He put the note asking him to come to the carousel at the bottom, and found the pad of sticky notes.

On a whim, he wrote three notes:

SORRY

REALLY

SON

He pasted them throughout the room, and hoped his mom would understand.

JJ walked out of their hotel room and closed the door behind him.

Off to the carousel.

AFTER TALKING TO the chef, Penny left the kitchen feeling both excited and frustrated. On the one hand, they'd ruled him out as a suspect, so that was good. And JJ seemed to have cleared his mom, but other than that, their investigation was at a standstill.

Penny didn't like this part of being a detective. In her dreams, she was the one who solved the mystery easily, and made her grandpa proud. And then maybe everyone would finally see her as someone other than a small girl who liked to read.

Maybe they'd finally see her as a budding detective.

Penny was so lost in thought that she almost ran into her grandpa.

"Ah, good," the detective said. "I was looking for you."

This didn't sound good. Penny could tell by his tone.

Her grandpa cleared his throat. "I spoke with your mother."

Uh-oh. Penny tried the casual response. "How are things in Florida?"

"You can cut the chitchat, kiddo." He sounded grumpy. "They know we're stuck here. And that there was a murder. They want you staying as far away as possible from all this. That means no more investigating, you hear?"

"Okay," Penny said.

Her grandpa sighed. "Just stick to your books."

But she had no intention of stopping. Her parents were all the way in Florida. They didn't need to know what she was up to. Penny would just keep her detective work a secret.

"I'm serious," her grandpa said. He had a nose for liars—he was a detective, after all. "Hang out in the library. Once the snow lets up, we'll go home."

Outside, the snow was falling in big fat flakes, like it was mocking the detective.

Her grandpa muttered something under his breath, then left Penny in the den.

Penny clutched her copy of *The History of the Barclay Hotel* close to her chest. Maybe there was something in there that could help them, like a clue about Mr. Barclay. Maybe reading was the answer to this investigation.

She settled into one of the big chairs by the warm fireplace, enjoying the feel of the pages between her fingers.

Penny stumbled upon information about Mr. Barclay's daughter Constance when she reached chapter five. It stated that Mr. Barclay was a very private man, and that he kept his daughter from any reporters and press. There were no pictures. But the book did list the year she was born; quick math put Constance at age twenty-four.

Penny paused. A woman at the age of twenty-four, that could be . . .

She was about to grab her notebook when there was a strange sound. Something was . . . rolling. On the old wood floor.

Penny looked down and saw a marble. It rolled until it hit her book bag.

There was a giggle. Penny picked up the marble and looked around. There had to be a kid who wanted it back, right? It was a nice marble, older and heavy, like it could be from decades ago.

"Hello?" she called. But there was no reply. Just silence and a waft of cold air.

She thought she heard more rolling—another marble. Penny tried to chase the sound, but it just faded. Like it was never there. Almost like that cat in her dreams . . .

Penny pocketed the marble and sat down by the fire. She picked up her book from the coffee table. Where was she . . . ?

But before Penny could get back to reading, a note fell out of the book.

Meet me at the Barclay Carousel as soon as possible.

Penny jumped from her chair and looked around. She hadn't seen anyone who could've left it. Some stealthy

messenger. Or maybe someone had put it there at breakfast earlier in the day.

She remembered her grandpa's warning. No investigating.

Of course, *technically* she wasn't investigating. She was
just going to the carousel.

Maybe there was a clue there. Or maybe it was JJ or
Emma, trying to keep the investigation going (despite
those meddling adults).

Penny tucked her book under her arm, and hurried to
the carousel room. She was a detective, and she was ready
to solve the mystery.

36

JJ **ARRIVED AT** the carousel at noon, and it was very dark. Someone had closed the shutters on the windows, so all you could see was a sliver of snow outside. JJ looked for a light switch but couldn't find one.

"Hello?" JJ called. His voice echoed. He waited, then began walking around the carousel. Maybe whoever invited him here had left already.

The carousel looked like it was old enough to belong in a museum. The horses were hand-painted, and had decorative saddles. There were several in a row, then a carriage (for the parents, JJ guessed), all with fancy, colorful artwork.

He wondered if this carousel could be haunted. He so

wished he had time to set up his equipment . . .

JJ stepped onto the carousel, and ran his hands along the saddle of one of the painted horses. In that moment, he wished he could see the carousel in action.

It was as if someone had read his mind.

Suddenly, the lights came on in the room. That was creepy. And the music started as a *wah-wah* weird electronic sound and went to a full-on carousel song. The carousel began moving, faster and faster. JJ could feel the air whirling around him, and he had to hold on to one of the horses so that he didn't fall over.

He tried to move, so he could step off. But the carousel kept moving faster.

Faster. And faster still.

JJ caught a glimpse of a dark figure out of the corner of his eye, standing near the control panel. But the carousel moved too fast for him to get a good look, and the person had turned their back so he couldn't see who'd started the carousel.

The carousel showed no signs of slowing down. JJ was sure something was wrong with it.

He had to hold on to the horse with both hands now. Everything around him was a blur, even the dark figure, who was now leaving through the heavy wooden doors.

"Help!" JJ called. But his screams couldn't be heard over the loud, delirious carousel music.

JJ used his legs to steady himself. Then he moved from one horse to the next, until he was at the edge of the carousel. The centrifugal force (he remembered from science class) was even more powerful on the outside of the platform.

He looked to the floor, and knew he had to jump if he was ever going to get off this thing.

This was going to hurt!

JJ closed his eyes, and took a breath. He imagined he was jumping into a swimming pool (it seemed like a more comforting image than the hard, cold floor).

And he screamed at the top of his lungs. Maybe it was for courage, maybe because he was insanely afraid.

But he jumped.

37

JJ HIT THE wood floor on his side, sort of. He was pretty convinced he'd bruised his shoulder and twisted his right ankle.

The music finally slowed. And so did the carousel.

Penny came running over. "JJ? What happened?!"

JJ sat up, rubbing his shoulder. "Someone started this thing and set it to self-destruct. Or, more accurately, JJ-destruct."

"I managed to turn it off, but the speed was set to max. You're never supposed to do that," Penny said.

"No kidding." JJ stood, trying to keep his weight on his left foot. The carousel had come to a complete stop now. "I got a note." He pulled the paper from his backpack. He felt sort of stupid now; he'd walked right into this trap.

"I got the same one," Penny said, waving a piece of paper. "I think we were both supposed to be on the carousel, but I was late."

JJ said, "This invitation to the carousel was a trick to get us here."

"Right." Penny thought of the rolling marble. It had delayed her just enough to keep her from the carousel. "I was lucky, I guess."

"Me, not so much." JJ winced as he tried to limp toward the door.

"It means we're getting close to catching the killer, JJ. They know that we're onto them, and they're trying to scare us off." Penny rushed ahead of him. "We have to keep going."

JJ thought about his mom grounding him, but it suddenly seemed less important now that he had a killer on his tail.

"Come on," Penny said. "I know how to narrow our suspect list."

"What do you mean?" JJ asked, limping as quickly as he could to keep up with Penny.

"Mr. Barclay had a daughter. And I think she's the missing clue."

38

IT TOOK JJ and Penny forever to make it back to their secret room because of JJ's twisted ankle.

When they finally arrived, JJ groaned as he sank into one of the big club chairs. "This ankle is sadly the least of my troubles right now." He told Penny about his mom learning that she never got the letter from the principal, and about being grounded in the hotel room.

Penny said, "I can help you. Tell your mom I'll tutor you over the computer—parents love it when you're being proactive."

JJ smiled. Penny was right: his parents *would* love that. Maybe that was his ticket out of one mess. Plus, maybe they could talk ghost hunting. Penny was a smart researcher, and JJ knew it was good to have a skeptic on your team. "Thanks, Penny," he said.

When Emma showed up, she apologized for storming off. JJ and Penny filled her in on the conversation they had with the chef about his alibi and what happened at the carousel. "Hot dog! Are you okay?"

JJ showed her his ankle. Truth was, it had been pretty scary. "This killer is getting nervous."

"We have to be onto something," Emma mumbled as she took a long look at the list of suspects on the wall. When she got to her uncle, she put a big fat X next to his name. "The police will probably need to see his phone records, but I think we can bump him off the suspect list. No opportunity, because he wasn't here."

"That theory rules out my mom too," JJ said. "What are the chances that she'll un-ground me when she hears about that?" He doubted it, but he hoped that knowing she wasn't a murder suspect anymore would at least make her happy.

"What about everyone else?" Penny asked.

"That leaves Ms. Chelsea, Buck Jones, and Fiona

Fleming." JJ thought about what else they knew about the three of them, but he came up empty. "All we know is that they were each here on Friday morning around ten thirty. They have motive and opportunity. But as far as the means go . . ."

"Well, the killer brought the poison, and apparently, you can buy it on the internet pretty easily," Emma said, her voice trailing off. "Oh, I almost forgot, I found this letter in Mr. Clark's room."

"You broke in?"

Emma shrugged. "I got us a new clue." She handed Penny the letter.

"*I know who you are,*" Penny read aloud. "*You will pay.*" She handed the letter to JJ. "It's signed *His Daughter.* Who is that?"

"No idea, but *you will pay* sounds like a pretty big threat. Someone was mad at Mr. Clark." Emma tacked the letter to the wall under EXTRA CLUES.

"What if it's Mr. Barclay's daughter, Constance?" Penny asked. "I've been reading *The History of the Barclay Hotel*—there is a lot about Mr. Barclay that could be important to our investigation. For instance, Mr. Barclay was always very kind to everyone he had business dealings with. So the way he was behaving on the morning of his death just doesn't add up. And then there's his daughter. There's not much in the book about her. It said that Mr. Barclay protected her privacy like crazy—I haven't even seen a picture yet, just her name and the year she was born, more than a couple of decades ago. So she has to be pretty old by now, right?"

"I don't get it," Emma said, sounding irritated for no apparent reason. "How is ancient history going to help us find a killer in the present?"

"Mr. Barclay's daughter would be about twenty-four years old," Penny replied. "What if she's one of our suspects? Both Ms. Chelsea and Fiona are the right age. They could just lie and use a different name, right?"

Emma hesitated. Then she shook her head. "If she's mad at Mr. Barclay, why send a threatening letter to *Mr. Clark*?"

"Emma's right. That doesn't add up," JJ chimed in.

Penny was a little insulted that her new friends just

shrugged off her thoughts about Mr. Barclay's daughter. It was a real clue, right?

JJ added, "What I don't get is, if the killer wanted Mr. Barclay dead, why didn't he or she just give him a cupcake with peanut butter in it? Mr. Barclay was allergic to peanuts."

Penny nodded. "That's true. It's even in the book."

The room went silent as the three of them realized that they were stuck.

"My grandpa is right," Penny said, standing up. "We need to find out more about our victim."

JJ agreed. "Let's find out more about Mr. Barclay."

PENNY TOOK A peek inside the dining room. Everyone was still having lunch. The guests were spread so far out amongst the tables that you might think they were worried about contracting a deadly disease from one another.

Ms. Chelsea and Fiona Fleming (sitting at separate tables) were both reading: Ms. Chelsea was lost in her Agatha Christie mystery novel, and Fiona was reading what appeared to be a theater script. The cowboy looked grumpy, clutching a cup of coffee like his life depended on it.

JJ's mom sat alone, making notes on a notepad. Penny's

grandpa also sat alone, stroking his mustache, like he was thinking.

Mr. Clark, Penny noticed, was not in the dining room or at the reception desk. She took the opportunity to take a look through the glass of the double doors to Mr. Barclay's office, but it was very dark and deserted inside. She left and walked toward the kitchen. When she got closer to the double doors to the kitchen, she heard voices and decided to see if the butler might be in there.

When Penny got closer to the voices, she realized it was the chef and Mr. Clark arguing. She froze.

"I cannot keep your secret for much longer, monsieur," the chef pleaded. "The kids were asking me about it earlier, and one of the guests implied I was a murderer! *Moi!*"

"Calm down, Pierre." This was Mr. Clark talking. And that British accent was gone again.

Penny felt like the puzzle pieces that didn't seem to fit were shifting, and she could see things making sense now. Maybe, possibly . . . Could what she thought be true?

"I don't like it," Chef Pierre said, but he sounded less upset. "Please, monsieur. Tell them the truth."

Mr. Clark said something Penny couldn't understand, and then there were footsteps, the kind that could only be made in fancy dress shoes.

Penny tried to turn and find a place to hide, but it was too late. Mr. Clark was already through the double doors, smacking her right in the face.

"Ouch!" Penny yelled, and jumped back.

"You." Mr. Clark pointed at her. "Were you eaves-dropping on our conversation?"

"No, I wasn't," Penny argued. But clearly she was.

This argument really was beside the point because, more importantly, Penny had a hunch. She studied Mr. Clark's face, looking for a clue to her new theory that would make everything add up.

"A straggler, that's what you are," Mr. Clark said. He grabbed Penny by the elbow and guided her toward the dining room. "Let's get you back to your grandfather."

In the dining room, everyone looked up as Mr. Clark and Penny entered.

"Detective," Mr. Clark said, letting go of Penny's elbow now. "I believe you lost your granddaughter. I caught her snooping around the hotel."

Penny looked at Mr. Clark's face. The time to prove her theory was now or never. She had to be brave. She had to be bold.

Penny reached out, and pulled at Mr. Clark's mustache.

There was a gasp from the back of the room (must've been from Fiona Fleming). Penny held up one side of the handlebar mustache (which looked an awful lot like a fuzzy caterpillar), and exclaimed, "This is not Mr. Clark."

It was like the handlebar mustache was the glue that was holding the whole disguise together. Now that it was gone, Mr. Clark's whole face was falling apart! His fake nose started peeling off, his eyebrows were coming unglued, and now that Penny got a closer look, she was pretty sure that hair was a wig.

JJ jumped up from his spot next to his mom. "No way!"

"Fiddlesticks," Buck Jones muttered.

Mr. Clark reached for his nose and tried to patch it.

But then JJ came running up and took a swipe at the wig. He stepped really close to Mr. Clark. "This isn't Mr. Clark."

Penny nodded. "It's Mr. Barclay."

40

THE ROOM WAS silent for a few beats, then it was chaos, with everyone erupting in questions.

Why did he . . . ?

Where was he . . . ?

What in the world!

Why was I suspected . . . ?

WHY DID MR. BARCLAY LIE?

"Everyone, please." Mr. Barclay peeled away the last of his disguise, then sat at one of the dining tables. "Allow me to explain." His voice was deeper now, calmer. And the fake British accent was gone.

Mr. Barclay had pretended to be the butler, Mr. Clark, all this time. But why?

Mr. Barclay said, "Last week, on Friday, Mr. Clark ate a cupcake that I believe was intended for me. The police were still determining cause of death, and I knew that the only way to catch the killer was to pretend that he or she had succeeded. And to bring the suspects here to my hotel."

"So, if it was Mr. Clark who actually died," Ms. Chelsea said, more to herself than anyone else, "that means that everyone here is no longer a suspect, right?"

Mr. Barclay shook his head. "The cupcake was intended for me."

"I must say you are quite the actor, Mr. Barclay," Fiona Fleming interjected. "But why pretend to be Mr. Clark?"

"I was clearly the target. I thought if I pretended to be Mr. Clark that I would buy myself some time. We used to trade places for fun from time to time." Mr. Barclay sighed. "I'm very sorry he was the victim of a crime that was intended for me."

Detective Walker cleared his throat. "Perhaps now is the time for me to get involved."

"I'd say so," Ms. Chelsea piped up. "You're the detective."

"*Retired*," Detective Walker said. "If you remember, I came here for a nice weekend away."

"We all did," JJ's mom said. "But maybe it's time we caught this killer."

"And my mom has an alibi!" JJ called. All eyes were on him all of a sudden. He explained how the chef was on his phone on his way into town, and had an alibi. And then how his mom was on the phone around the same time. "There's no reception here, so the only way both the chef and my mom could have been making a cell phone call at the time of the murder was if they weren't on the premises."

His mom nodded and smiled. "That's right!"

"Nice work, young man," Detective Walker said. Then he turned to Mr. Barclay. "I'll need to speak with you about the events that transpired on the day of Mr. Clark's death. *Privately.*"

Mr. Barclay nodded, and stood.

All the adults were arguing with each other, but Penny was quiet. Something was still bugging her.

What if . . . Penny leaned closer to JJ. "I have an idea."

She thought about what her grandpa had said about the missing piece to the puzzle.

"I have an idea too," JJ whispered back. "What if Mr. Barclay wasn't the target at all?"

Penny nodded. "What if the killer actually wanted *Mr. Clark* dead?"

PART IV

MIDNIGHT AT THE
BARCLAY HOTEL

ONCE THEY WERE outside the dining room, JJ said to Penny, "We need more information on Mr. Clark."

"And Mr. Barclay." Penny then looked around. "Hey, have you seen Emma? We should probably fill her in on everything that just happened."

JJ looked too. "I haven't seen her in a while. Did you notice if she came downstairs with us?"

Penny shook her head. "I don't know."

"Maybe she's way ahead of us. Maybe she's already looking for more clues about Mr. Barclay and Mr. Clark," JJ said. The dining room was still loud with arguing adults—something he was happy to leave behind. "I have an idea to find out more about Mr. Clark."

"I'm going to find Mr. Barclay," Penny said. "Meet you in an hour, right here? And hopefully one of us will run into Emma."

JJ nodded.

The killer was after Mr. Clark.

Mr. Barclay said that Mr. Clark knew all his business dealings. That meant that Mr. Barclay had to have hired him.

If there was anything JJ knew from watching his mom run her business, it was that there was a lot of paperwork involved. Filing cabinets full of the stuff. And that meant that there'd be a paper trail.

Mr. Barclay had to have a record of hiring Mr. Clark, right? There had to be some information about Mr. Clark in there, like a former address, personal references, stuff like that.

JJ made his way to Mr. Barclay's office and was surprised to find it unlocked. And here he thought he might have to go hunting for the key! Today was his lucky day. His ankle even felt a little better, as long as he didn't put his weight on it.

JJ decided it was better to keep the light off. He'd just open the blinds a little, and let the view of the mountains stream in. Snow was falling outside and coating the trees and the lawn in front of the hotel. It didn't show any signs of letting up.

JJ focused his attention on the row of filing cabinets against the back wall. He opened the drawers, one by one. Accounting records, something called deeds (whatever that was), and a bunch of other stuff JJ didn't need.

But the bottom drawer finally had him hitting the jackpot. There it was: *Gregory Clark*. The folder was the same as the others: gray and bland. Only it was different in a not-so-good way.

The folder was empty.

JJ searched the rest of the cabinet, to see if maybe there was another folder, anything else to go on.

It was right there in the bottom drawer, waiting to be discovered. JJ's heart beat a little faster as he read the words.

Last Will and Testament. The letters were small and the text boring legal stuff, so he scanned the pages.

JJ halted somewhere on the third page of the document, where a name was printed in bold letters.

JJ held his breath. He read the name twice, just to be sure.

Then he clutched the papers and rushed out of the office.

He had to find Mr. Barclay, and fast.

WHILE JJ WAS trying to find out more about who Mr. Clark was, Penny decided it was time she talked to the man who'd been pulling all the strings, setting up this whole murder mystery weekend.

Mr. Barclay. He had to be done talking to her grandpa. So where was he *now*?

Penny looked at the map. Most adults loved the hot tub, but Mr. Barclay might want some quiet. She took a peek inside the library, only to find it deserted.

She tried the Cupcake Shoppe, and found Mr. Barclay sitting in the dark, in a booth in the far corner of the small bakery.

"Mr. Barclay?"

The man was slumped over, his hands clasped on the table. He stared off into space. Penny remembered her dad having the same stare when her great-aunt died.

"It's me, Penny?" she said, not sure if he remembered who she was.

Mr. Barclay looked up and smiled, still looking sad. "Oh yes, the straggler. You remind me of my daughter when she was your age," Mr. Barclay said out of nowhere. "Always looking for the next fun thing to do."

"Where did she move to?" Penny tried to sound casual but wasn't sure if she'd achieved that. What if his daughter was right here at the hotel, and hated her father's guts for some reason? What if Ms. Chelsea or Fiona Fleming was really Mr. Barclay's daughter?

"My daughter is dead, Penny."

"Oh. I'm sorry." So much for that being a lead. Penny sat across from Mr. Barclay. "What happened?"

Mr. Barclay's voice was very sad, and crackled like one of those old vinyl records her mom liked to play. "Her mother had a rare genetic blood disease, though she passed away quick. My daughter had the same disease.

But her death took a few years—I tried every doctor, every medicine . . ."

Penny looked around the Cupcake Shoppe. Most of the seats were wrapped in plastic, like moths in a cocoon. "You built all this for her?"

He nodded, looking very sad again. "She was too sick to leave the estate. So I tried to make the hotel fun for her."

"I think that makes you a great dad," Penny said.

Mr. Barclay gave a small smile in response to the compliment.

"I actually came to ask you about Mr. Clark," Penny said. "How did he become your butler?"

Mr. Barclay seemed to collect his thoughts. "Mr. Clark came to the hotel last year after I'd spent over ten years in a daze. After my daughter died, I was a mess. I needed a butler, so I placed an ad for the job. Mr. Clark called within a day, showed up the next, and did a great job from the start. I didn't ask any questions."

Mr. Barclay continued, "I always loved the theater and games. One day, to cheer me up, Mr. Clark dressed as a magician. The next day, a gunslinger. I joined in on the fun after a while. It was easier to pretend to be someone else than to be myself."

"That disguise you wore today was pretty advanced," Penny said.

"Thank you."

An idea was forming at the back of Penny's mind, one that would make a lot of puzzle pieces fall into place. "Did Mr. Clark teach you that?"

Mr. Barclay nodded. "Gregory was quite the expert in disguises. He once dressed as Chef Pierre. I didn't even know it was him."

Penny said, "A couple of the suspects mentioned that they met you that Friday, and that you went back on some agreements you made. The cowboy guy and his ranch, the librarian and her grant, and JJ's mom with the restaurants."

"That *was* quite odd," Mr. Barclay agreed. "Mr. Clark told me they all despised me, that death threats had been made. It's how I knew who to invite this weekend: Mr. Clark told me. And I never talked to anyone that Friday morning. Mr. Clark dealt with them all, he said."

Penny asked, "Could it be that Mr. Clark was disguised as you, telling all those people to go away?"

"But why?" Mr. Barclay asked, looking confused again.

"You said that Mr. Clark knew all your business dealings," Penny said, trying to formulate the butler's motive. "What would happen if you died?"

Suddenly the door to the Cupcake Shoppe flew open.

JJ barged in, looking out of breath. "Mr. Barclay." He waved a stack of papers. "You have to read this!"

JJ RAN OVER to where Penny and Mr. Barclay were sitting and said, "I have something you need to see."

He dropped the stack of papers on the counter of the Cupcake Shoppe in front of Mr. Barclay.

"Why young man, I was just talking——" Mr. Barclay started to say.

But JJ wasn't going to be interrupted. "You'll want to read this. It's your will."

When Mr. Barclay took too long, JJ flipped the pages. "Look! It says here that he inherits everything."

Penny had no trouble reading the name even though it was upside down: *Gregory Clark*.

Mr. Barclay went pale. "This is not my will. I mean,

this is not a will I created. But this signature here at the bottom is mine."

JJ looked triumphant. "I'll bet Mr. Clark faked it."

"But he's dead now," Mr. Barclay said. "What does it matter that he inherits everything?"

JJ had no answer to that.

Penny felt an idea come together in her mind. "What if Mr. Clark dressed up as you, got a new will made that says that he gets everything you own and all your money, and then fake signed it. And killed you. Only he didn't get a chance to kill you, since someone murdered him first."

Penny's theory was starting to make a lot of sense.

Mr. Barclay mulled that over. "I don't understand. Why would someone other than Mr. Clark then try to kill *me*?"

Penny said, "They didn't want to kill *you*. They were after *Mr. Clark*."

The question was: who?

PENNY AND JJ left Mr. Barclay in the Cupcake Shoppe, still holding the forged will.

"We're so close to solving this mystery, I can feel it," Penny said.

They made their way back to the library and found Emma roaming the stacks. "I've been looking for you guys! Did you find any more clues?" she asked, eager to do something.

JJ and Penny went up the spiral staircase to join Emma.

"Mr. Barclay is alive," JJ said.

Emma blinked and smiled. She was crying big fat tears of joy. "I'm so glad. He's like . . . a father. So wait— who is dead then?" She wiped her eyes.

"Mr. Clark." Penny told her about what they found out about Mr. Clark and the fake will.

"I'll bet his name wasn't even Gregory Clark," Emma said.

"That's brilliant, Emma," JJ said. "What if Mr. Clark's other identity is that of an *actual* con man . . . ?"

Emma's face brightened. "That con man you guys told

me about, the one that Detective Walker said was in the area. Whatshisname . . ."

"Gerrit Hofstra," Penny said. "What if Gerrit Hofstra was pretending to be Mr. Barclay?"

Emma nodded. "If he was acting as Mr. Barclay the Friday of his murder, it would certainly explain Mr. Barclay's sudden change in character, how Mr. Barclay kept going back on his promises with everyone."

Penny finished her thought: "It was this Gerrit Hofstra, impersonating Mr. Barclay. He sent everyone away. And he faked that will, so he could get all of Mr. Barclay's money."

Emma looked determined. "We should go update our files in the secret room."

JJ hesitated. "I was going to review the ghost hunting footage from last night."

"I'll come along," Penny said. "We have a bet, remember?" She wasn't about to let JJ review the ghost hunting footage on his own. Penny wanted to see it with him, to add a skeptic's perspective.

Emma was feeling left out and a little hurt by that. But then again, she'd messed with the camera, so she figured they'd be done reviewing in a few minutes anyway. Emma left, after telling them, "I'll see you guys soon, then."

Penny tried to do her best to contain her excitement about reviewing the footage. She was the one who didn't believe in ghosts. Right?

"Let's see what we have," JJ said. He wanted to see if he'd caught the infamous lady in white, or that kid who supposedly haunted the hotel.

He said as he grabbed the camera, "It's infrared footage, so it may not—what?" The camera casing was cracked! What happened?

"Oh no," Penny said. She was genuinely upset. "What happened to the camera?"

"I don't know." JJ checked the memory card. Thankfully, that was still intact. The camera had run out of battery power, but then it had been almost twenty-four hours since he'd set it up. "Let's see if the memory card is still functioning."

Penny and JJ found a seat at the small table near the

window. JJ plugged the camera's memory card into his laptop.

Penny had to remind herself not to hold her breath. For someone who didn't believe in ghosts, she sure was excited to see the footage. But then after the disappearing cat, the kid with the marbles . . . It was hard to stay a skeptic.

JJ opened the file and let it play. First, he saw himself setting everything up. That was boring, so he ran the video faster, to get to the good stuff. He wanted to see what those hours of ghost hunting had produced a little quicker.

"What are we watching? This is just footage of us," Penny said.

"Wait," JJ said.

JJ started to notice dust particles in front of the lens that looked like they were dancing.

And suddenly, they saw a white image appear.

Penny sat up straighter in her chair, eyes wide. "Is that . . . ?" Penny was too afraid to finish her question.

JJ nodded. "I think so." It was a ghost.

"I guess I'm losing my bet. That's a ghost." Penny was afraid to blink as she watched the footage. The white shape took on the appearance of a human.

"Wait," JJ mumbled. "I'm talking to this ghost." That was weird. Was it a person after all? But no, the shape was hazy, just like he'd seen in real ghost hunting footage done by the professionals.

Who was he talking to?

He thought back to that moment, and remembered more clearly now: *he'd been talking to Emma.* Penny began to realize it too. "Emma," she said.

Emma, who had appeared out of nowhere.

Emma, who avoided high fives. Who wouldn't go into Mr. Barclay's office . . .

Emma, who seemed to disappear at random times.

It all made sense now.

JJ and Penny looked at each other and then said at the same time, "Emma is a ghost."

JJ KEPT HIS eyes glued to the footage until the camera battery drained. Emma was coming into view again as the camera shut off.

Penny exhaled. Their new friend was a ghost.

JJ's camera battery should have lasted longer, but being zapped of energy was a classic sign of a haunting. Emma had drawn the energy from the camera, in order to make herself appear.

"Who was Emma?" Penny asked. "I mean, if she's a ghost."

"She's tied to the hotel somehow." JJ opened his backpack and grabbed the *History of the Barclay Hotel* book he'd been avoiding this whole weekend.

"I read some of it," Penny said. "But not all." Chapter twenty-three covered the entire Barclay family tree. Both Penny and JJ pored over the pages, until they both caught a familiar name.

Emma.

JJ read aloud, slowly, "Mrs. Barclay passed away from a rare genetic blood disease at the age of thirty-four. Not long after, the Barclays' daughter was diagnosed with the same affliction. She died just after her twelfth birthday. Although her first name was Constance, Mr. Barclay's daughter preferred to go by her middle name, Emma."

Penny said, "I talked to Mr. Barclay. He built the fun stuff in the hotel for his daughter because she was too sick to go anywhere." She hesitated, because she knew this proved ghosts exist. "Emma is haunting the hotel."

Penny reached into her pocket for the marble. She knew it had been given to her by a ghost, when she was in the den and JJ was on the runaway carousel.

JJ closed the book and jumped when he realized Emma was sitting right across from them. As much as ghosts can sit, anyway.

"Hi, Emma," Penny said. She felt nervous.

"I guess you know now," Emma said to Penny and JJ. She sounded sad.

JJ asked, "Why didn't you tell us?"

Emma shrugged. "It was just so nice to have friends, and not worry about germs and nonsense. You know I haven't seen another kid in years?"

"That must get really lonely," JJ said.

Emma nodded. "You have no idea. My dad can't

see me. The chef can't either. All they see sometimes is flickering lights—I can do that, if I concentrate. Adults can't see ghosts. Only kids can. With the exception of Fiona Fleming—she must be a real psychic medium."

"Can you see the other ghosts?" JJ asked. He was a ghost hunter, after all.

Emma shook her head. "We can't see each other. I think my mom might be roaming around—in room two seventeen. That used to be her favorite because it over-looks the valley. It's where she died."

JJ asked, remembering what was in the *History of the Barclay Hotel* book, "What about the midnight hour—can you see each other then?"

Emma smiled and her eyes got misty. "No. But I can feel my mom, and sometimes I smell her perfume."

Penny asked, "Did you have a cat?"

"Oh yes, a black one," Emma said. "Her name was Chloe."

"So, she's a ghost cat," Penny said. And she'd tickled her feet. In room 217.

JJ tried not to be too amazed by the fact that he was

sitting across from a ghost. This was what he'd been hunting for this entire time, after all. "Oh my gosh, I have so many questions. I'll start with the one that has to do with our investigation. Couldn't you spy on people to find out who killed Mr. Clark?"

She shook her head. "It's not that simple. Plus, I can't go inside Dad's office, or the dining room. When I was still . . . alive"—Emma paused—"those two rooms were off-limits. So now that I'm a ghost, they're off-limits too."

"JJ?" The door to the library opened, and JJ's mom popped her head in through the doorway. "If I remember correctly, I grounded you."

JJ froze. *Uh-oh.*

His mom smiled. "But since you're in the library, reading . . . Hi, Penny."

"Hi, Mrs. Jacobson," Penny said.

JJ's mom pointed a thumb over her shoulder. "It's dinnertime, you two."

"We're coming." JJ turned to look at Emma. But of course, she was gone.

JJ, PENNY, AND JJ's mom walked into the dining room, and it was a sight to see.

Each of the suspects was sitting at a different table, with Mr. Barclay at his own table too. It looked like the loneliest dinner party in history.

"Well, this is depressing," JJ's mom said as she sat at Mr. Barclay's table.

Penny glanced around the room, looking for her grandpa.

"Where's Detective Walker?" JJ's mom asked, as if she was reading Penny's mind. "He wouldn't skip this meal— he's been talking about the veal since we got here."

"No veal, I'm sorry to say," Mr. Barclay said. "With

all this snow trapping us here, the chef had to resort to breakfast foods."

As if on cue, Chef Pierre swung open the doors pushing a dinner cart that was holding a serving plate piled with waffles, alongside trimmings like strawberries, whipped cream, and chocolate. JJ and Penny sat up. This was a kid's dream meal.

"I still don't see my grandpa," Penny muttered before digging into her food.

Mr. Barclay seemed to be looking for the detective as well. He checked his pocket watch. "I spoke with Detective Walker just an hour ago."

Penny felt a sense of dread, but said, "I think I'll go look for him. JJ, guard my waffles until I come back." JJ nodded with a mouth full of food.

She left the sad dining room, and she headed for the basement of the hotel, thinking that she'd find her grandpa relaxing in the pool or hot tub. But both were deserted, the bubbles of the hot tub just on standby under the water's surface.

This was odd. Where could her grandpa have gone?

The library was empty (no Emma, either—Penny could've used a friend), and so was the carousel room. Penny still got the shivers when she thought of how that thing went totally bananas.

But her grandpa was nowhere to be found. Not even in the Cupcake Shoppe or the bowling alley.

Penny's search ended in the den, the one that over-looked the white landscape. It was dark, but the moon-light reflecting off the snow was brightening the room. Snow was still coming down, almost as if to tell Penny that she was never leaving the Barclay Hotel. Not that she minded. But she sure would feel better if she could find her grandpa.

She walked closer to the big window and peered out-side. Penny had looked all over the *inside* of the hotel, but what if Grandpa was *outside*? She scanned the snowy landscape outside and saw the faintest set of footprints. Normal, adult-size ones but also really big ones with toes pointing outward, like they belonged to a big man.

Or rather: to a man in cowboy boots.

What if Buck Jones was the killer, and he'd lured her grandpa outside? He could freeze to death out there.

Penny looked down at her flimsy tennis shoes, ones that were better suited to Florida sun than Colorado snow. There wasn't even time to grab a coat or gloves or a hat. If her grandpa was outside, she had to get to him, and soon. Penny knew she had to be brave.

She opened the door. The top of a snowdrift sprinkled onto the wood floor. She got slammed in the face by the cold and the relentless falling snow. She stepped outside, feeling the flakes quickly coat her skirt as she trudged her way into the knee-high snow.

Penny followed the footsteps, but then they started to disappear. Snow whirled around her like a vortex. And for a split second she saw the hazy outline of a tall, lanky man. The man was dressed in overalls, looking like an old-timey photograph. He was pointing toward the maze.

It was the ghost of Mr. Roberts, the old caretaker of the Barclay estate. Penny had read about him too in *The History of the Barclay Hotel*.

Penny took her eyes off him for just a second to blink, and when she opened them again, the ghost man was gone.

This could be dangerous. She'd read about the Barclay maze. How back in its day, the maze got guests confused, leaving them lost and wandering for hours. In her summer sneakers and without a coat, this could be a death trap.

But if her grandpa was already in there, the maze was definitely a death trap!

Penny took a deep breath and reminded herself again that this was the time to be brave.

She entered the maze, trying to make sense of the jumble of footprints. She put her hand on the outer wall of the hedge maze—she knew that was one way to make sure you could find your way out. She had read it in a book somewhere, back at the library in Florida.

Florida, where it was something like seventy degrees outside. Penny shivered. Her fingers were quickly going numb as she touched the hedge maze.

Penny walked along the perimeter, until she turned a corner. And there was her grandpa!

The detective was slumped on the ground. His head had a red wound, like someone had smacked him with a hard object. Her grandpa's eyelashes had tiny icicles on them—he'd been out there awhile.

"Grandpa," Penny said. She used her icy hands to tap his cheeks. "Wake up!"

The detective didn't respond.

Penny felt herself panic. "Grandpa!"

46

IT TOOK A few smacks to the cheeks, but Detective Walker finally opened his eyes.

He groaned. "There are no ghosts." Detective Walker was in a daze and thought he'd seen Mr. Roberts, but when he tried to wake up, he had just fallen back into the darkness that was caused by the blow to his head. Now he tried to sit up. "Poppycock," he said.

Penny didn't think that now was the time to argue. She knew what she'd seen, and she knew that the Barclay Hotel's ghost groundskeeper, Mr. Roberts, had probably saved her grandpa's life. "Someone whacked you in the head, Grandpa." Penny stood. "I'll go get help."

"No." The detective's voice was faint. He was slowly

coming back to consciousness, so he stood, rubbing his head. "The killer thinks he got me. Let's see how he reacts when I come to dinner."

Penny and her grandpa brushed off the snow. "Do you know *who* hit you over the head?" Penny asked.

Her grandpa said, "I don't know who was out here, but I was following footprints in the snow. Large ones."

Penny nodded. "Like cowboy boots."

"That's what I was thinking when I started following them. Nice detective work, kid. That was very brave," he added.

"I want to be a detective, like you," Penny said. "I can do it."

"I know you can." Her grandpa smiled. "I'm proud of you, Penny. But now I'm going to clean up and get some veal."

"And catch a criminal," Penny said. It was a bit cheesy, but true. "Oh, and I should probably warn you, there's no veal."

"What's for dinner, then?" The detective looked grumpy again.

"Waffles. Come on, let's go," Penny said. Her feet were frozen.

"That's if we can find our way out of this maze," the detective said, rubbing his head and wincing.

Penny smiled and said, "It's easy: follow me."

PENNY AND HER grandpa rejoined the dinner party (which still didn't feel much like a party). Mr. Barclay had made all the guests sit at the same table, even though everyone looked pretty unhappy about it.

Dinner was a quiet affair. The waffles were magnificent, Penny thought.

After everyone finished eating, the detective cleared his throat. "I found out some new evidence today. I spoke to one of my colleagues using the landline. She confirmed that our murder victim is actually Gerrit Hofstra, a famous con man from the Netherlands."

"Penny and I had already figured that out!" JJ exclaimed.

Penny smiled. She was feeling pretty smart.

"Where's the Netherlands?" Fiona Fleming asked, ignoring JJ. "My geography is a little stale."

Detective Walker said, "Near Germany, north of Belgium and France. In any case, he'd been stealing fortunes from unsuspecting rich people all over the world, before he came to Colorado."

Mr. Barclay said softly, in a sad voice, "He was trying to con me out of the Barclay estate." It had to be hard to realize that the person you trusted most was out to con (and kill!) you.

The detective nodded. "It seems Mr. Hofstra would befriend a wealthy landowner, someone with a similar height and build to his, so he could disguise himself and change the will. Then . . ."

They all knew what this con man had planned to do next. Murder, is what.

"Well, then maybe it's good that he's dead," the cowboy said. "He sounds like a horrible man."

Everyone looked at the cowboy.

"But I didn't kill him!" Buck Jones pushed his plate aside.

"That's what all guilty people say," Fiona Fleming shot back.

And Ms. Chelsea just gave everyone a librarian stare, which she usually saved for loud people in the library.

Things were heating up. The question was, of course: who wanted Gerrit Hofstra dead?

THERE WAS ONLY one place to go to continue the investigation: the secret room. JJ and Penny left the dinner party, and hurried there together.

"We have to find Emma," Penny said as they made their way through the wardrobe entrance.

JJ agreed. "Every good idea we've had has come from working together."

And it was as if Emma thought the same thing, because she was already in the secret room, pacing past the suspects' pages on the wall. She was a ghost, but so what?

"It's down to the librarian, the cowboy, and the actress," JJ said.

Emma smiled. "Well, hello to you too."

"Hi." JJ paused.

Penny did too. She wanted to say something about the whole Emma-being-a-ghost business, but she didn't know what.

As if she had read their minds, Emma said, "We can talk ghost stuff later. Right now, we have a murder case to crack."

Penny smiled and felt at ease. It was time to get down to business.

"We're close, Emma. I can feel it," JJ said.

Penny began looking at the evidence. "We have stuff to add."

She told Emma about her grandpa and how someone whacked him over the head, leaving him to freeze to death outside. "And there were footprints outside, large ones. Like the kind that might be made by cowboy boots." She scribbled the evidence below the cowboy's suspect page. "I still don't know why he would want Mr. Clark, that is, Gerrit Hofstra, dead."

Emma said, "But he wanted Mr. *Barclay*—my dad—gone, right? It's so confusing."

JJ stepped back.

He felt just like he did when he was reading: confused and overwhelmed. They needed less. Just the facts, without the suspects and motives that were all about Mr. Barclay and not about Gerrit Hofstra.

JJ moved to the wall and took everything down: the suspects' pages, the sticky notes, everything. Then he tore a page from the notebook and wrote: *Gerrit Hofstra*. "We have to look at everything fresh. Forget about Mr. Barclay—it's this con man who wound up dead."

Penny felt a jolt of energy from this new perspective. "What about the clues?"

Emma was excited too, so excited that she managed to send a bunch of sticky notes flying with her ghost wind. She laughed. "Well, I guess we can pick up the clues."

"That's a great idea," JJ said. "What clues still connect to our fake butler, Mr. Clark?"

Con man was one clue.

Script another—even though that one originally belonged to Fiona Fleming. Mr. Clark liked the theater.

That threatening letter—another clue—was in his room.

"There's only one suspect who makes these clues connect," JJ said.

Emma nodded and said, "Fiona Fleming. She wanted to do this murder mystery play."

Penny frowned. "But why would she want *Gerrit Hofstra* dead?"

JJ muttered, "The answer has to be here somewhere."

Penny remembered the ghost hunting they had done in the library, and how those scripts fell down right in front of them. Including one particular script, with that list of cast members. As if the ghost who knocked down those plays wanted to show them. Emma's mother, perhaps. Penny smiled and went for the door. "I know where it is!"

JJ and Emma followed her, after glancing at the suspect wall one last time. "Where?"

"In the library."

48

EMMA DID HER disappearing act as they left the secret room, but appeared again in the library by the time Penny and JJ arrived.

Penny immediately started scouring the bookshelves on the second level. "It's a long shot, but—here it is! Scripts."

JJ and Emma joined her, wondering what Penny had in mind.

"Mr. Clark, or Gerrit Hofstra, liked disguises," JJ said, catching on to her thinking now. "You think he was an actor in a play?"

Emma looked at the scripts section. "These are pretty old, but not this one."

"That's the one I was looking for." Penny grabbed the play. "*Midnight at the Barclay Hotel*, by Fiona Fleming."

Penny turned the front page to look at the actor line-up. There he was: Gerrit Hofstra.

Hofstra was listed as playing Mr. Barclay.

JJ said, "But he wasn't listed as Mr. Clark, his fake identity. He was listed as Gerrit Hofstra. That means—"

"Fiona Fleming knew who he was," Emma said, finishing his thought. "She knew that Mr. Clark was actually Gerrit Hofstra, the con man. But if she exposed him like this in the play, why kill him after all?"

"I don't know." Penny closed the script. "We should go ask her."

"Good idea," Emma said. "But if she is actually the killer, won't she be dangerous? How will you stay safe?"

JJ pondered that as they left the library. "I might have an idea . . ."

THE THEATER WAS dark when JJ and Penny got there.

"You think she'll show?" Penny asked JJ in a whisper. The acoustics in the theater were excellent, so everything you said sounded like a foghorn unless you kept your voice way down.

They stood near the stage. Waiting for a killer. Emma was off to roam the hotel, to see if she could find the actress, while Penny and JJ set what they hoped would act as a trap.

"I don't know," JJ whispered back. "We could be waiting for nothing."

They had gone up to the theater lighting control booth to set up JJ's ghost hunting camera. Thankfully he'd been able to repair it. Only the lens had a crack down the center. Even though it was designed to catch ghosts, it would do just as well catching a living person. Along with a voice recorder that JJ had in his pocket.

Maybe they could catch Fiona Fleming, trip her up, and have her confess to the murder as JJ and Penny questioned her. That was the plan, anyway.

Penny sat on the stage, dangling her feet.

"You think she could be hiding backstage?" JJ asked

Penny. He walked up to the stage and climbed on. JJ was about to go behind the curtains when there was a loud clanging sound.

Suddenly, there was a spotlight on Penny and JJ. They covered their eyes against the bright light. Up in the control booth there was the faint outline of a woman.

Penny called, "Fiona?"

She didn't respond at first, but then asked, "Why are you kids here?"

"To talk to you." JJ blinked. When he looked up, Fiona was gone.

He hoped she hadn't found his camera.

Penny looked for Emma, but she was a ghost. Literally.

A minute later, Fiona came out from backstage. "Shouldn't the two of you be with your mom and grandpa? It's after eleven already. Don't you have a bedtime?" Her words and demeanor were sharper than usual, and not so bubbly. It was all an act, that nice actress they'd seen this weekend. Now, here onstage, Fiona Fleming looked like a snake ready to bite.

"We're here for the truth," Penny said, undeterred by Fiona's attitude.

"Oh, *now* someone cares about the truth!" Fiona threw her hands to the sky in an overdramatic fashion.

"Yes, we want the truth about you," Penny countered. She stood up.

Fiona lowered her arms. She blinked.

"We know who you are," JJ said.

She looked puzzled.

"You wrote that threatening letter to Mr. Clark," JJ continued. "You are 'His Daughter.' From the letter."

Fiona's face softened. She looked sad. "I am," she said. "I *was* a daughter. But not anymore."

The theater was dead silent.

Fiona cleared her throat. "My father is dead. The butler was the one who killed him."

"MR. CLARK, MR. HOFSTRA—whoever he pretended to be," Fiona went on, waving her hands while stepping closer to JJ and Penny. "He killed my father."

You could hear a pin drop.

"Get away from her!" Emma called from somewhere in the audience seats.

Penny tried to find her, but the lights were so bright. They were cornered by Fiona, onstage.

Fiona said, "I see you brought your little ghost friend Emma. Is she here to help you?"

Ignoring Fiona, Penny said, "We found this in the library." She held up the script. "It has Mr. Clark's real name in it, Mr. Hofstra. You knew he was a con man."

Fiona smiled. "Leave it to the little kids to figure it out."

"We're not little kids," JJ mumbled. But he felt cornered, just like Penny. Both kids stepped back, out of the spotlight.

Fiona continued, "Yes, I knew Mr. Hofstra. He was my father's butler, in Chicago. He weaseled his way into Dad's life, just like he did with Mr. Barclay. Only my father wasn't so lucky. He died of a heart attack—or so it looked, anyway."

"You think your dad was murdered?" Penny asked.

"I couldn't prove it, but . . . yes." Fiona sighed, then got agitated again. "He was poisoned, but the killer made it look like a heart attack. And Gerrit Hofstra forged my father's will and took all his money. My dad was a wealthy man, like Mr. Barclay."

"How did you know to come here, to Aspen Springs?" JJ asked.

Fiona stood in the spotlight now. It was like she'd been waiting in the wings until it was her turn to tell the truth. "After he died, I searched my dad's computer for evidence and found that someone had been researching the Barclay family. My father barely used his computer, so I knew it wasn't him."

Fiona turned, and stepped out of the light. She was choosing her words carefully.

"I wanted revenge. I wanted Hofstra to pay. But I knew I needed a plan to take down a con man like him."

"So, you moved here," JJ said, prodding her to say more. He sure hoped his recorder was getting this.

Fiona nodded, and turned back to JJ and Penny. "I set up my theater company in town, knowing that Mr. Barclay loved murder mystery games and theater. I approached him, after I had the company up and running."

"And Mr. Barclay said yes to your play." Penny got closer to Fiona, slowly.

Fiona smiled. "The truth is, I was actually pretty excited to host a murder mystery at the hotel. But I was here for Hofstra, so I wrote him into the story."

This was a clever plan, Penny thought. Not that she was about to say that out loud.

Fiona gave Penny and JJ an evil smile. "That Friday, I

had an appointment with Mr. Barclay. But I knew how Hofstra liked to use disguises. Don't get me wrong—he was good—but I knew it wasn't Mr. Barclay I was speaking to on the phone. Then I brought the poison I ordered ahead of time, and drove up to the Barclay Hotel. All I needed was ten minutes alone with Gerrit Hofstra . . ."

There was an uncomfortable silence. Was Fiona about to confess to the murder?

Fiona took a deep breath. "When I arrived, I met Mr. Barclay, but I knew it was really the con man who killed my father. Then I followed him into the kitchen, where there was a perfect cupcake, waiting for Hofstra. When he looked away, I quickly poisoned the frosting on the cupcake. It was frighteningly easy, really.

"Then I got the invitation," Fiona went on. "And I knew I had to come here for the weekend, to make sure no one suspected me. Unfortunately, Mr. Barclay did . . ." Her face clouded over.

"How about the other suspects?" Penny asked.

Fiona smiled again. "This was where I got lucky. There were four other suspects! The chef, the cowboy, the librarian, and your mom, the CEO. I couldn't have written it better in the play."

JJ paused, thinking of all the danger they had been in that weekend at the Barclay Hotel. "The elevator, the carousel . . ."

Fiona nodded and shrugged, in a "you got me" way. "When I figured out that the two of you were on to me, I knew I had to stop you. It was pretty easy, honestly. The elevator is old, and I just had to turn up the speed on the carousel. Only that didn't scare you, did it?"

"A little," JJ admitted.

Penny shot JJ a look that said "act brave!"

"And I almost got rid of your grandpa out there in the blizzard," Fiona said to Penny.

Penny felt anger boil inside her as she thought of how her grandpa could've frozen to death outside in that maze. But she had to keep her detective calm.

Penny realized they'd need a full confession, one for

the murder. She said, "So that Friday, at ten thirty, you just poisoned Mr. Clark and left."

"Mr. *Hofstra*," Fiona said, correcting Penny.

"You killed him."

Fiona nodded. "Yes. And good riddance."

This was it: the confession they had been looking for. And they had it all on tape!

50

PENNY FELT A rush of excitement. She'd just gotten the killer to confess, like a real detective!

Now they had to make an exit . . . JJ was glancing around too.

Uh-oh. This was going to be harder than they'd thought.

Penny looked for Emma, but their partner in detecting was nowhere to be found. Penny was starting to get panicked now, just like when she went scuba diving.

JJ was scared too, but they had to stall so that they could keep Fiona talking. He said, "But Mr. Clark—err, Hofstra—he was a killer first."

Fiona nodded. "Exactly." She paused and her eyes

welled up. "My father was my best friend, you know? He was always there for me, even when I messed up."

JJ knew a thing or two about that. His mom and dad always had his back, even when things were not going so well, like with this whole failing-class business. "You felt like you had to kill Mr. Hofstra," he said.

Penny was beginning to panic big-time now. Fiona was a killer!

Fiona continued, "I forgot that Mr. Barclay had the script, which would be evidence of my guilt. So when the invitation came, it seemed like the perfect opportunity to get rid of the one piece of evidence that could be my downfall. It was a chance I couldn't resist. But when I searched Mr. Barclay's office, the script wasn't there."

JJ said, "It was in the library. Mr. Barclay has a whole collection of scripts."

Fiona nodded, and exhaled. "Of course, why didn't I think of that?"

There was a definite shift in the mood of the room. It felt colder, icier even than the air in the maze just hours earlier.

Penny stepped back. She clutched the script.

But Fiona stepped closer. "I'll take that script now."

"No!" Penny yelled, and turned away. But Fiona lunged and tried to pry it from her fingers.

Penny tried to hold on, but Fiona was too strong. She snatched the script, leaving Penny holding just a few strips of torn paper.

Fiona hurried offstage. There was a rumble, and then a *swoosh* sound.

Penny and JJ stood together, onstage. Penny smelled perfume, strangely and out of nowhere.

"Look up!" Emma called from somewhere in the audience seats. JJ and Penny looked to the ceiling, only to see the stage light contraption up above them lowering.

No, it was *dropping*.

Right on their heads.

THERE WAS ANOTHER *whoosh*, a movement of
air. Penny and JJ felt themselves being pushed, but they
couldn't see anyone else there.

Penny was mesmerized by a white shape floating
around the stage.

But JJ was too busy looking up. Whoever (or whatever?
A ghost?) had pushed them out of the way of the falling
stage lights had saved them both. JJ's backpack got caught
on the end of one of the lights and was ripped right off his
shoulders. Penny had a scratch on her arm, but otherwise,
they were safe. And the ghost (of Emma's mom, they
guessed) was gone.

Luckily, Penny and JJ weren't the only ones with detective skills. It seemed like Detective Walker, Ms. Chelsea, JJ's mom, and even the chef had a hunch that something was up, because they all came running through the double doors at the same time.

Emma had warned them. She made the lights flicker all over the hotel. Although they couldn't see her, Emma managed to make a mess everywhere, sending papers flying (and even the potted plants), hoping they would follow. Thankfully, the detective did. And the other guests followed him, from their rooms all the way to the theater.

"What's going on?" Detective Walker asked as he got to the stage.

"Fiona Fleming is the murderer!" Penny called. "She's back there." Penny pointed backstage. "Be careful when approaching her, because she's very angry."

Her grandpa nodded. He went backstage, only to find Fiona wrapped in thick ropes, the ones that held back the theater curtains. Buck Jones was tying them.

Fiona screamed, "Let me go!"

Buck Jones said, "You need to be quiet, ma'am."

The detective smiled. "Nice lasso job, Mr. Jones." The cowboy did win that rodeo competition after all.

"I'm innocent!" Fiona called. "You have no evidence."

"Oh, I think we have plenty," Detective Walker said.

Penny added, "That script you're clutching, for one. Your motive is right there in your hand."

"Plus, we have your confession on tape," JJ said.

Buck Jones added, "And you stole my boots."

Penny said, "So that's how those prints ended up in the snow. That explains a lot!"

The detective led Fiona out of the theater, and everyone else followed behind them. JJ was clutching his broken backpack, while Penny couldn't stop smiling.

"That was very dangerous," JJ's mom said, scolding him a little. "Fiona Fleming is a murderer. What if she'd . . ." Her voice trailed off. It was too scary a thought to finish.

"I'm fine," JJ said, lying a tiny bit. His ankle felt extra painful, and he was shaking from the close call with the theater lights. "We caught the criminal."

"We did!" Penny said. They high-fived, because that's what you do when your team wins. Emma followed along, feeling pretty good about herself as well.

And Buck Jones sauntered off, happy to have his boots back.

AFTER FIONA WAS secured by the detective (he locked her in his room, then called his old partner for backup), everyone returned to the den to drink some hot cocoa. It was dark outside those enormous windows, but the moon was reflecting off the white snow on the ground.

"Hey, it stopped snowing," JJ said. For a moment, he thought he saw a tall shape, near the maze, but it was gone in the blink of an eye. The ghost of Mr. Roberts had caretaking to do.

JJ's mom smiled. "No more snow! That means we can go home tomorrow. Thank goodness, I have so much work to do." She seemed lost in thought for a moment, but then said to her son, "I did enjoy what little time we spent together, though, JJ. We should take a vacation more often. But next time, let's stay away from murder investigations."

"If it's a trip to a haunted hotel, count me in," JJ said. There were quite a few haunted Colorado hotels on his list, though he figured he should save that tidbit of information for another time. When you're a ghost hunter, you don't want to freak out your parents too much. Take that as a bit of advice from JJ.

"Maybe we hit the pool before we leave tomorrow?" his mom asked.

"That sounds great!"

"Nice work, kiddo," the detective said to Penny. "Brave, if a little dangerous."

"How can you be a detective if you're not a little brave?" Penny said. It was true.

"Maybe just don't tell your parents exactly how close those theater lights came to knocking you out," her grandpa said in a low voice. He was afraid they might never let Penny come visit again. And he really liked having her around.

JJ's mom checked her watch. "Well, it's late, so I'm

turning in. But I imagine you have some ghost hunting you want to do."

JJ smiled. "Maybe." Of course he did. A ghost hunter's work was never done.

As the adults all trickled out of the den to go to bed, Penny pointed to the grandfather clock. "Look, JJ."

JJ saw: it was eleven forty-five.

And there was Emma. Appearing out of nowhere as usual.

JJ said, "I say we stick around for the midnight hour."

"Me too," Emma said with a silly grin on her face. She did a cartwheel, then settled into one of the big chairs.

"Since you won our bet, I agree: let's see if any more ghosts show," Penny added. Clearly JJ was right: the Barclay Hotel was indeed haunted.

JJ brought out his ghost hunting gear, and set it up around the den. He handed Penny the EMF detector and sat next to Emma.

"You know that I'm all the evidence you need," Emma said, motioning to herself.

"I know." JJ hesitated. "But I figured you might not want people to know."

Emma nodded.

Penny plopped down into another chair, and pointed the EMF detector away from Emma. "Ready?"

Before anyone could answer, the grandfather clock chimed twelve. And the Beethoven tune filled the den.

THREE
MONTHS LATER

THE INVITATIONS WENT out on a Monday, because according to Mr. Barclay's new advisors (that would be JJ and Penny), it's the best day to invite kids to a party. Mondays can be hard, we can all agree on that, and kids need something to look forward to. The letters were printed on parchment paper, the kind that tells you whoever is throwing the party means business.

Two hundred invitations went out that Monday, perhaps a few more than that. Mr. Barclay wanted to make sure that every kid in Aspen Springs was invited. Buck Jones hand-delivered them to kids while riding his favorite horse. It took a while to get to everyone, because most kids wanted to pet Lemon Drop before they left.

Here's what the invitation said:

Dear Aspen Springs,

Congratulations! You are all winners. Come this Saturday to the Barclay Hotel for the Grand Reopening (expect surprises!).

There will be cupcakes and pancakes, horseback and carousel rides. You can get lost in the hedge maze, or in the library (the largest private library in Colorado!). Enjoy the newly renovated pool and hot tub (bring your parents!), or go bowling—there is a lot of fun to be had for all.

Bring your friends and friends of friends. All are welcome.

Sincerely,
Mr. Barclay

P.S. Despite the fact that there is a regular ghost hunting tour, the Barclay Hotel is not haunted. We promise.

Of course, JJ and Penny knew this last teeny tiny

written statement was not true, but, then again, they'd sworn to Emma that they'd keep her ghost status a secret. Emma was so looking forward to having a whole bunch of kids to hang out with.

And that morning, before the grand reopening, everyone was back. Well, everyone except Fiona Fleming. She was now incarcerated and directing the prison theater—*Midnight at the Barclay Hotel* was her first play. Rumor has it, Gerrit Hofstra's ghost is haunting the prison.

But at the real Barclay Hotel, there was no more murder. The rooms were clean, the carousel was properly serviced, and the pool's slide was ready for new guests to barrel down into the water. Even the hedge maze was freshly trimmed—miraculously so, overnight. Mr. Roberts might've had something to do with it. The ghosts at the Barclay Hotel were just as excited as the humans to finally have guests again.

"Hey, JJ," Penny called from the other end of the den. "Do you know what happened to the twelfth EMF detector?"

JJ and Penny were in charge of the ghost hunting tour, along with JJ's mom and dad. His parents were interested in the paranormal now too, once they figured out how exciting and fun ghost hunting is.

"I'll bet my mom has that one," JJ muttered under his breath. Jackie Jacobson was convinced she would catch the ghost of Mrs. Barclay. A few times, she'd accidentally caught Emma, which was pretty fun for JJ and Penny.

Mr. Barclay was checking up on the Cupcake Shoppe, which was fully stocked. And Chef Pierre was trying out new pancake recipes.

Buck Jones was outside, getting Lemon Drop used to the higher altitude for horseback rides that weekend. Once he realized that a candy shop and a horseback-riding stable weren't such a good mix (no one liked horse hair in their candy bag), he focused his attention on sharing his love of horses with kids.

Detective Walker decided to open up his own detective agency, with Penny as his assistant when she was visiting. He was now walking the grounds to see that the hotel was secure.

And Ms. Chelsea was busy setting up the library, along with an audiobook corner, which was quickly becoming JJ's favorite way to read. Reading was a lot easier when he could listen along to the words. Ms. Chelsea got her library grant and decided that instead of an arcade, a giant slide, and a train, she would spend the money on an amazing kid hangout.

JJ managed to pass his classes, with Penny's and his parents' help. He was relieved that it was summer now—no school, and no more snow for a while.

Mr. Barclay walked into the den, looked out the big windows toward the driveway, and sighed.

"Are you ready, Mr. Barclay?" JJ asked him.

"Two hundred invitations." Penny whistled through her teeth. "That's a lot of kids."

Mr. Barclay smiled. "It's about time this place was filled with children's laughter," he said. "I miss it."

JJ and Penny could see Emma standing right next to her dad. She had a proud smile on her face.

"I can feel her presence sometimes, you know," Mr.

Barclay said softly. "And her mother's. Right here in the den."

"I think we can too," Penny said with a smile to JJ and Emma.

Mr. Barclay perked up when he saw the first bus pull up the long driveway. It was full of children, plus their parents. "Here they are," he said.

The first ghost hunting tour was at eight that evening, and everyone was ready—JJ, his parents, Penny, Detective Walker, and of course, Emma.

The buses unloaded, and kids were piling out.

"Stragglers," Emma said with a grin.

"So many stragglers," JJ said.

Mr. Barclay smiled. "Stragglers are my favorite kind of guests."

ACKNOWLEDGMENTS

If you read the book before these acknowledgments, you probably figured out that I really, *really* love mysteries. And I owe a bit of thanks for that to a librarian. As a kid, I was an overzealous reader who'd read most children's books at our library when I discovered Agatha Christie's mysteries at the suggestion of a librarian. I've been hooked ever since. I don't remember the librarian's name, but I will thank every librarian now—there aren't enough pages to express how important you are, the times you had just the right book, or how often you made me feel at home when I was the new kid in town. Thank you.

When I finished writing this book, I wasn't sure anyone would get what I was trying to do, but Laurel Symonds did. I couldn't be more grateful you're my agent, Laurel. I'm one lucky writer.

Kendra Levin was another person who got it—thank you for making sure the Barclay Hotel found a home at Viking. I hit the jackpot twice, because Aneeka Kalia took over as editor. This book wouldn't be what it is without you, Aneeka.

Copyeditors catch all those last mistakes (and tiny plot holes...): thank you, Janet Pascal and Laura Stiers, for your sharp observations.

It's one thing to imagine the story in your head; it's a whole other (mind-blowing!) thing to see it illustrated. Thank you, Xavier Bonet, for bringing these crazy characters to life. Thank you to the art department and Jim Hoover for making this book look so good.

Being a writer is a lonely job sometimes, but my friends always get it too. Thank you to SCBWI, Mystery Writers of America, Sisters in Crime, and Pikes Peak Writers for always giving me a place to find comradery and learn new things. My best writer pals Deb, Jenny, Laurel, Ali, Nicole, Mary, and Pam and Sarah—thank you for listening, and for cheering me on.

Last but never least: thanks to my family, for supporting me when I'm off writing or daydreaming, and for going with me to the library. It's where all the cool people are, you know.

Fleur Bradley is passionate about two things: mysteries and getting kids to read. When she's not active in her local SCBWI chapter, she's speaking at conferences on how to engage reluctant readers. Originally from the Netherlands, she now lives in Colorado, not too far from the historic (and haunted) Stanley Hotel.

You can find her at ftbradley.com and on Twitter @FTBradleyAuthor.

Xavier Bonet is an illustrator and a comic book artist who lives in Barcelona with his wife and two children. He has illustrated a number of middle grade books, including the Thrifty Guide series by Jonathan Stokes and Michael Dahl's Really Scary Stories series. He loves all things retro, video games, and Japanese food, but above all, spending time with his family.

Visit him at xavierbonet.net and follow him on Twitter or Instagram @xbonetp.